DEADLY
INDEPENDENCE

DEADLY
INDEPENDENCE

Laura Pauling

Redpoint Press

paperback ISBN-13: 978-1512092790
paperback ISBN 10: 1512092797

Summary: After discovering a body during the fireworks, it's up to
Holly with the help of her friends and her dog, Muffins, to solve the
murder before the killer decides it's time for Holly to meet her maker.

Edited by Cindy Davis

for all mystery lovers

HOLLY PIPED THE last of the red frosting onto her cake design. The magnificent colors exploded. A special design she'd worked on for weeks. Something never done with cheesecake—not that she'd seen.

With a satisfied smile, she snapped a picture of these last few cakes. The base was a solid piece of strawberry cheesecake. Above it were the fireworks, pieces of white cake with red, white, and blue frosting. They resembled the explosion of color that would light up the sky tomorrow night.

Weeks before the Fourth of July, she'd woken in the middle of the night. A dream had sparked the idea. Immediately, she'd worked in her kitchen until dawn broke. She'd made the first one. Now, after several weeks of filling custom orders, exhaustion settled on her.

It was a good feeling, a sense of accomplishment.

The fireworks celebration was in less than twenty-four hours, and to complement her cake design, she planned on hand selling mini-cheesecakes, each decorated with their own explosion of color made up of raspberries, blueberries, strawberries, and kiwi.

Her business, *Just Cheesecake*, just might make it. Even after Millicent, the daughter of the owner of her competition, *The Tasty Bite*, had done everything possible to ruin her cheesecake business after the murder in the small town of Fairview.

Muffins whimpered at her feet.

"Don't worry. I haven't forgotten about you." She held her fingers down to the small gray dog and let him lick off the frosting. "You've been so patient." She'd been busy filling and delivering orders. Muffins had often been left behind. "I'll make it up to you. Promise."

Someone knocked on the door.

Holly smiled. "Come on in." She grabbed two tall glasses and filled them with iced tea. The ice cubes clinked, reminding Holly of the searing temperatures lately.

Charlene entered, eyed the glasses, then glared suspiciously at Holly.

"What?" Holly asked.

Charlene seemed surprised whenever Holly knew her friend was coming. But Charlene had proven to be a good friend, despite her crankiness, and stopped by enough that Holly stayed permanently prepared for company. The older woman shuffled across the floor. Today, her usual flyaway hair was damp from a shower. Her rumpled shirt was untucked, and she still wore her yellow rain boots.

"How do you do it?"

"What?" Charlene snapped. "Don't you dare mention a thing about my boots."

Holly held up her hands. "Fine. Fine." She'd heard the explanation before. Charlene claimed her feet stayed cooler in the insulated boots than wearing sandals. "Iced tea?"

"I suppose it would be rude to say no." Charlene sat at the small kitchen table and sipped. "A little sweet. But it'll do." She drummed her fingers on the table, then ran them up and down the side of the glass.

"Okay. Spill it," Holly ordered.

"I don't know what you're talking about. Can't a woman be tired after being worked like a dog for days?"

"Definitely." Holly understood. After they solved a murder together and Holly had been invited into Charlene's secret society of amateur sleuths, Holly had returned the favor and recruited her friend to help through busy seasons. "I'm near exhaustion too."

"Pfft. How old are you—fifteen? You should have an endless supply of energy."

"Try twenty-two." Holly pulled out a tray of chilled mini-cheesecakes from the fridge. Maybe something sweet would lighten Charlene's mood. The past week she'd been extra cranky.

"Fifteen. Twenty-two. Same thing." Charlene nibbled on one of the tasty cakes then grumped some more. She finished it off, then eyed Holly. "I see what you're trying to do and it's not going to work."

"Oh, really. And what's that?"

Charlene tapped the side of her nose. "Old Charlene knows everything." She fell silent, then added, "If you wanted me to put in a good word with my son, all you had to do was ask."

Holly gasped. Charlene had been teasing her about Trent since they'd met. "That is not why I offered you iced tea and your favorite cheesecake."

"Then why?" Charlene asked.

How could Holly tell her that she knew why her friend had been unusually cranky, other than being overworked, as she claimed? Instead of what she felt was the truth, Holly said, "It's because you're my friend. And I appreciate you."

"Stop right there. No mushy stuff. I don't even like you. Very much."

Holly pushed another tiny cake toward her. "Sure. Don't worry. I know you like me. I know your life was completely boring until I came to town." A different realization hit Holly. Maybe Charlene was lonely? Maybe she used the secret society as a crutch? Her husband had passed away years ago. Holly would have to think about that—and look around for a suitable beau.

"I stopped by to see if you'd solved the problem we're going to have tomorrow night."

"Sure did." Holly brightened. "You'll find out tomorrow night. That's all I'm going to say for now."

Charlene grabbed another mini-cheesecake. "Well, if that mystery is solved, I'll be going. Don't want to wear out my welcome." She shuffled back to the door but paused, her hand on the knob.

Holly waited, allowing time. She'd figured out a few days ago the reason behind Charlene's restlessness.

"Fine. I'll admit." Charlene kept her back to Holly. "We need a good mystery to solve. I'm bored."

"We could go shoe shopping," Holly offered.

"Absolutely not." Charlene moved on through the door.

"I found a pair of flip-flops you'd love. All sparkles and glitter."

Charlene responded by slamming the door, then yelling, "Keep up that nonsense and you'll have to hire new help."

"See you tonight!"

***

"WHAT'S THE BIG surprise?" Kitty asked, her eyes alight with excitement.

Kitty was one of Charlene's closest friends, along with Ann. Together the four of them solved mysteries together, or talked about mysteries.

In the factory-style production line Holly had organized, Charlene mixed the pre-made cheesecake filling and poured the batter into the tins. Holly pulled them out of the oven, and she and Ann were in charge of topping them with berries. The final touch was a drizzle of sugar glaze. Kitty's job was to place the cooled mini-cheesecake tortes into plastic containers, and then place those in boxes.

Holly smiled and flashed her a look that said, you'll have to wait and see. She couldn't wait to reveal her big secret. Plus, she had a bonus surprise for all of them.

"Don't bother," Charlene said, elbow-deep in the next bowl of batter. "Not only is she keeping us up at all hours of the night, but she's not saying a word."

"Soon. Soon," Holly teased. "Let's get this last batch done, first."

"Slave driver," Charlene muttered.

Kitty closed another box of cakes. "Oh, you just stop it. Holly's been the best thing to happen to us and this town since the summer we cracked the mystery of the exploding trashcans."

"What?" Holly placed the last of the strawberries on this batch of cakes. "Exploding trashcans? Please, tell. Sounds mysterious."

Ann opened another package of fresh berries. "It was Officer Trinket's first job, his first year on the police force, and he was bound and determined to figure out why the trashcans down at the lake were tipped over every week, trash strewn everywhere."

Holly giggled. "Sounds like a tough one."

"It might not have been murder, but it was more exciting than being stuck in the kitchen."

This cutting remark made Holly fall silent. Normally, her feelings would be hurt, but she could tell something was bothering Charlene. If her theory of Charlene needing a little love or male companionship was right, then she'd have to talk to Trent first before she tried to match make.

Ann offered her an apologetic smile for Charlene's rude comment.

When they put the last of the containers in the box, Holly couldn't stop the smile from spreading at the sight of the packed boxes, filled with tortes to sell the next night at the fireworks. From what she'd heard, no company, not even *The Tasty Bite* had ever attempted hand selling. And why not? Holly thought it was brilliant. One more way to boost her business and get her product out there.

"Okay, wait here." Holly headed to the back storage room. Earlier, she'd stored a special batch of chocolate chip cheesecake bars, just for this moment. She also had a small cooler filled with chilled fruity wine.

Her friends' eyes grew wide at the treats.

Holly poured the wine into plastic wineglasses and passed them out. "My way of saying thank you. I don't know what I would've done without the support and friendship of you three."

They toasted and cheered and polished off the food. When the last drop of wine disappeared, Holly cleaned up. "Ready for the big secret?"

"Finally," Charlene stated.

"I thought you liked a good mystery," Holly teased, hoping to lighten Charlene's mood and erase the scowl.

Charlene chose not to respond but deepened her scowl.

With a sigh, Holly said, "Follow me." She led her friends out to the back parking lot, behind *Oodles*, the charming restaurant next door, and *Gotcha*, the boutique gift store. *Just Cheesecake*, her shop, was nestled between them.

A warm breeze cooled the dried sweat from hours of baking. The stars twinkled, tiny lights across the heavenly canvas. Holly loved it. She hadn't told anyone, but her favorite activity lately, was sneaking out at midnight and lying in the grass to stare up at the sky. Just her and Muffins.

The parking lot was empty except for their cars and a white van. Her friends looked around, wondering.

Holly stifled a laugh. "What do you think?"

"Um, it's great, Holly," Ann said.

Kitty scratched her head. "Wonderful."

Charlene gave her a suspicious look. "I want to know where you got the money for it? I've been helping you with the books. Remember? So what bank did you knock off to buy this beauty?"

Holly shrugged. She'd still had her secret savings account from her previous life, and she hadn't yet shared her past with Charlene. Not that she didn't trust her, but she had been waiting for the right time.

"Okay, fine." Kitty gasped. "I have no idea what you two are talking about."

Holly led them to the van and around to the other side. In bright colors, *Just Cheesecake* was printed across the side, along with the graphic of a cheesecake. "It's refrigerated."

For days, they'd debated how to transport the Fourth of July tortes over to the celebration, while keeping them fresh. Holly had taken an afternoon off after finding an ad for the truck online.

After congratulations and talk of the next night, Holly shooed her friends home to catch some sleep.

"Nothing can go wrong tomorrow night." Kitty patted her shoulder before they piled into Charlene's car.

Alone in the parking lot, Holly leaned against the van and stared up at the sky. She was doing it. Living her dream. Only when she was alone, away from prying eyes and caring friends, did Holly allow the pang of grief. Her dreams had come at a high price.

Goosebumps rippled across her arm. Even without Muffins, Holly sensed something wasn't right. She wasn't alone.

She straightened and peered into the darkness. Maybe she should have left with her friends.

Again. The sound of shoes scraping the pavement.

SHE DIDN'T HAVE a weapon, except for lipstick. That was it. She pulled it out and bent her knees, ready for anything.

Another step. From the other side of the van.

Better to surprise than be surprised. After slipping out of her flip-flops, Holly crept toward the sound. A darkened form disappeared just as she peered around the hood.

Pebbles bit into the bottoms of her feet. Ignoring the pain, she crept alongside the van and past the back end. The figure stood. Alone.

With a few quick steps, she came up behind the person and jabbed the end of her lipstick into their back. Her heart thundered. "Ready to meet your maker?"

"Holly?" The figure turned.

Relief flooded through her and then a burst of anger. "What're you doing? Scaring a girl to death in a parking lot late at night?"

Trent played innocent, like a schoolboy, acting surprised to see her out at this time of night with his wide-eyed expression. His sandy blond hair appeared darker than usual, and shadows hid his eyes. He narrowed his eyes, with a hint of a smile. "Is that lipstick?"

Holly tucked the tube back into her pocket. "Maybe."

"What exactly did you plan to do with it, if I'd been a real threat?" Trent used a scolding tone. "Give me a makeover?"

"Hadn't thought that far." Holly stepped back, aware of how close she stood to him. "It wouldn't have happened if you hadn't been so sneaky."

"Sorry about that." He shifted, then changed the topic. "I hear you've been busy."

"I do run my own business." Holly hated feeling defensive, but after the scare, the adrenaline was fading, leaving her a bit grumpy.

"Right. How's that going?"

"Fine." Even though, through the fiasco of footprints in the frosting, she'd suspected him of crossing the line, working for the bad guys, she knew better. He was a good guy. Lately, he'd been busy with police work, and she'd been up to her ears in cheesecake. She let out a deep breath. "Sorry, it's been a long day."

"Thought you might want an escort home." He offered his arm. "Do you have to close up?"

"I'm all done." Escort her home? This had Charlene written all over it. "Your mom has great intentions, but I'm fine walking across the road." She found her flip-flops, then threaded her arm through his and they started back toward Main Street.

"You know my mom. She looks after her friends."

Holly agreed. Maybe a little too much. "About your mom..."

"What?"

At the road, they looked both ways, even though the town was deserted this time of night. Holly said, "Has she seemed grumpy to you?"

He laughed. "Isn't she always?"

She remained quiet in her thoughts until they were at her door. "I mean, grumpier than usual."

Trent rubbed the scruff on his chin. "Maybe a little more than usual. Not sure. Honestly, I've been busy with paperwork, and I don't see her every day."

"About that. When did you move out?"

"A year ago. Why?"

If Charlene had been used to living with someone, all of a sudden being on her own, even with a zillion cats, might be lonely. "I think your mom needs to date."

"What!" Trent exploded. "Date?"

"What? She's been a widow for a while now, and with you moving out, she could use companionship."

"No way." Trent straightened, determination pulsing off him. "She's got me and her cats and her friends."

"It's not the same." Holly should let it go, but Trent's reaction only made her more determined. Sometimes children were the last people to understand their parents were people with needs, apart from being parents.

15

"My parents had the love of a lifetime. No one could replace my dad."

"I'm not saying anyone could. But it's been years. Finding love again doesn't mean replacing your father in her heart. It's moving on. It's healthy." The more she thought about it, the more she felt Charlene would benefit from dating. Or at least thinking about it. She could lose the boots, too.

"Healthy? Considering you make cheesecakes for a living, you're not one to talk about health."

Holly spluttered out a laugh. "Love and cheesecake are two different things."

"Now you're talking love? Dating to love? Just like that."

"Whatever," Holly muttered, now fumbling with her key. "Thanks for the escort. Don't think I ever would've made it home without you."

He gripped her arm. "I mean it, Holly. Leave my mom alone. Don't push this idea of yours on her."

She flipped around, jerking away in the process. "I know. I should stick to my cheesecakes and not care about my friends when I see they're lonely."

"For the last time, my mom's not lonely."

"Sure. Whatever you say, Officer Trinket." She slipped inside and shut the door before she said something she'd regret.

Seconds later, he banged on the door. "You're invited to my mom's Fourth of July picnic, tomorrow. Three o'clock."

"Great, thanks!"

Holly slumped against the door. The last thing she'd wanted was a fight. Determination rose inside her. Regardless of Trent, she'd keep her eye out for a suitable match for Charlene.

***

MORNING CAME FAST. Bright streams of light invaded Holly's bedroom, piercing her eyes. She groaned and rolled the other way. Muffins yipped on the floor by her bed, needing to be fed and walked. Pressure and excitement for the coming day, her big venture at the fireworks celebration, selling her latest creation, woke with her, a steady companion. Holly's fight with Trent, the explosive words and emotions tripped through her mind. Her loyalty and concern for Charlene niggled at her.

It was too much.

With a sigh, she threw the covers aside. "I can't hide in bed all day, can I?"

Muffins barked his approval. Either that or he was starved for attention.

Even with a full day ahead, Holly decided to lavish some much-needed attention on herself and Muffins. She picked him up and snuggled. "How about a vanilla latte and a long walk? Will that be good?"

He yipped and jumped from her arms, heading to the door.

She laughed. "Okay, okay. But we need to eat, don't we?" For a brief second, Holly was thankful the door was locked. No way could Muffins escape. No way would she be seen in public again, in her pajamas. She'd carefully chosen a patriotic outfit for later, but for now, she slipped into jogging shorts and a T-shirt. The day would be a scorcher, unrelenting heat and humidity. By evening, the temperature would be perfect for chilled fruit tortes.

After a quick breakfast, she latched the leash to Muffins' collar. "Let's go, boy. Shall we?"

Forgoing the latte, Holly purchased an iced coffee from *Oodles*. The storeowner stood behind the counter this morning. A lovely lady with big everything. Big personality.

Big hair. A big laugh. And most importantly, a big heart. "Good morning, Lindsey!"

"Morning to you, sweetheart. Ready for a boiler today?"

Holly raised the ice-cold plastic cup. "Now I am."

Back on the road, Holly led one way while Muffins tugged to go in the opposite direction. His way led to a certain bakery she tried not to walk past. His way reminded her of the body found in her shop just a couple months ago. She fought off a shudder.

Muffins tugged again, barking.

"Fine. Fine." Guilt over spending so much time preparing for the Fourth might have had something to do with her giving in to him.

Holly tried to think about everything else but her competitor. She thought about *Just Cheesecake*. She thought about the coming night. She thought about Charlene and Trent. But, unfortunately, not thinking about Millicent and *The Tasty Bite* didn't stop it from coming into view.

The Tasty Bite was an adorable bakery. Holly wished she could spend more time in it, but Millicent and her habit of writing slanderous articles against her, kept her from entering. The owner, Millicent's father, Pierre, seemed to be a nice man. After a glance around, Holly decided to walk casually past the shop. Take a peek at her competition. Customers came in and out, carrying their baked goods and coffees. Casually, Holly dropped the leash.

Muffins sat there, panting.

The one time Holly wanted him to run so she'd have an excuse to chase him, he chose to obey. "Figures." She picked up the leash and headed to the bakery window. As she approached, a feeling of dread washed over her.

Bright colors from holiday baked goods sat in the window. Their latest creation featured cake, a combo of cheesecake and regular cake, in the shape of a fireworks display. It was a custom order design. Available for cookouts and barbecues.

The sick feeling turned into one of anger. Somehow, Holly knew, this had to do with Millicent. Holly had slaved over the design. No possible way could they both have created the same thing—which meant Millicent had played dirty. Spied and stolen. Probably without Pierre even knowing.

Abruptly, Holly turned and walked home. Gone was her casual morning of relaxation before a big night. Even though her design had done well, how much business had she lost to *The Tasty Bite*?

Probably a lot.

Holly spent the day cleaning her house. She washed and scrubbed and polished every room, floor, and cupboard. Not one speck of dirt was left anywhere. Not one cushion or blanket was out of order. Not one dust bunny lay forgotten under the couch or in a corner.

Unfortunately, the cleaning spree helped a little, but by afternoon, time to shower and get ready for the night, Holly was still in a mood. After showering and dressing in her white capris and tank with a sparkly sequins flag on it, she looked in the mirror.

Time for a pep talk.

"You can do this. You're only beaten if you let them get to you. Be happy. Smile. Focus on your customers."

By the time she arrived at Charlene's, Holly was thirty minutes late. When she parked and strolled to the front door, with forced cheer, her fake smile quickly faded at the sight of Trent sitting on the front steps.

Waiting.

PLASTERING ON A GRIN, Holly strode toward the house, determined to nod hello and find her friends, Charlene, Kitty, or Ann. Her other goal was to avoid Millicent. Not for the first time, Holly wished Millicent wasn't so interested in pursuing the life of a mystery novelist. The mystery book club would be more appealing without the appearance of her nemesis.

As much as she wanted to give no more than a cursory, polite look at Trent, her gaze lingered. His faded jeans and patriotic blue T-shirt set off his eyes and sandy hair. He'd be much easier to dislike if he wasn't so...available. Right age. Single. Cute. Then she remembered last night.

She nodded hello, hoping to walk past.

"Good evening, Holly. Can we talk?" He sounded humble, contrite, friendly.

Holly's upbringing brought her to a halt, but it didn't prevent her next comment. "No plans to sneak up and startle girls in the dark of the night?"

His smile weakened. "That's not fair."

"Life isn't fair, Officer Trinket."

He kept his calm. "All set for tonight?"

"Yes."

In the following silence, she felt bad for giving him a hard time, but after the day she'd had, she said nothing. Forgiveness wasn't on the menu.

"My mom can't stop talking about the splash *Just Cheesecake* will make tonight at the fireworks. Selling patriotic desserts. Great idea."

"Thanks."

"You seem to have a knack for business. Great vision for your company."

"Are you surprised?" she asked, accusation in her tone.

He captured her gaze. "Not at all."

23

A hint of a smile broke out on her face at his subtle reference to all the pain and aggravation she caused him nosing around in his murder investigation. She'd do it again in a heartbeat.

"You know what else I'm good at?"

"What?" he asked, hesitant and wary.

She tossed her hair over her shoulder. "Knowing when my friends are lonely."

He opened his mouth to respond. A flush crept up his neck, giving away his feelings.

"Have a good night." Holly waltzed past, ignoring when he called her name. She was in no mood for a lecture.

Charlene's backyard was filled with the smells of the grill and the sounds of friendly chatter and laughter. Charlene manned the grill, and Kitty and Ann were refilling chip bowls on the picnic table. A pang of loneliness hit Holly. Yes, some of these people were her friends, but she missed her family, her traditions. Was she assuming Charlene felt lonely just because she did?

"Holly," Trent said behind her. "I don't want to fight. Just talk."

She pretended not to hear him, her conscience digging at her. "Kitty! Ann! Do you need help?"

Kitty, obviously frazzled, cheeks red from the heat, hair frizzing, smiled in appreciation. But then, she looked past Holly. "No thanks, darling. We've got this covered."

Holly pushed her way to the table. "No, really. Let me help."

"I would, except"—she leaned close and whispered—"I'm under strict orders." Then she went back into the kitchen.

Ann shrugged and smiled.

Charlene called from the grill. "Glad you two could finally make it. About time, Holly."

Burgers sizzled, the smell tantalizing. Smoke billowed and flames shot skyward. Trent rushed over. "Mom, why don't you let me take over, before you set the place on fire."

Amused, Holly watched Charlene play tug-o-war with the spatula. Everything added up. Charlene asking Trent to invite Holly to the party. Kitty and Ann refusing her help. Charlene refusing to let Trent grill. This was a set-up. She sighed. This was one battle she lost the will to fight. On the way over to the grill, Holly grabbed a beer.

"Have something to drink." Holly held out the bottle.

Charlene gave her son a push then focused back on the grill, refusing to meet Holly's eyes. If Charlene played matchmaker, then Holly could return the favor. The last of her annoyance dissipated. Why let stolen ideas steal her fun? She didn't want Millicent to have that kind of power over her. Why let her friendship with Trent be ruined over a silly argument? Not worth it.

Trent almost bumped into her, stuttering out an apology. He accepted the drink with a hesitant smile. Holly jumped into conversation. She talked about the weather, the upcoming fireworks, and Charlene's cats. She talked about small towns, leash laws, and burnt burgers. She talked about anything and everything as the time slipped past. Every time Trent tried to start a conversation, Holly jumped in with more chatter.

At five o'clock, Holly exclaimed, "Look at the time! We ready, ladies?"

They cleaned up, leaving Trent in charge, and she grew excited and nervous about the fireworks.

He walked them to their cars. "Will you watch the fireworks with me? There's something I need to discuss with you."

Warmth rushed through her insides. A happy, giddy feeling. She quickly pushed it down. "I'll be busy. Working. I'm sure you understand."

"Sure do. I'll save you a spot anyway."

***

"ABSOLUTELY NOT!" CHARLENE turned away from Holly.

Kitty gasped. "I love them. What a fantastic idea."

"Traitor," Charlene muttered.

They stood outside the delivery van, near the celebration. Trays and trays of fruity and patriotic tortes filled the back of the van. Ready to be sold to hot and sweaty customers.

"It's not just a gimmick," Holly said. "These will make it easier for us to spot each other in the crowds." She held out the pink apron, emblazoned with the name brand of *Just Cheesecake*. "It will also help the crowd see us. Which will help sales."

"Fine." Charlene continued to grumble, then stopped. "On one condition."

Oh, great, thought Holly. She had a sneaky suspicion what the condition might be. "What?"

Charlene's eyes gleamed with victory. "That you watch the fireworks with Trent."

27

"I can't promise that. I might be working."

Charlene dug in, eyes narrowed. "Once the fireworks start, our work will be done. Promise you. All the selling that's gonna happen, will happen in the next couple hours." She pulled the apron over her head, but paused before tying it. "We have a deal?"

"Fine."

Holly ran over the plan for the night. Charlene would take the right, Kitty would cover the left, and Holly and Ann would walk through the center. When they sold out, more trays were in the van.

Before grabbing her first tray, Holly went to the driver's window. "Hey, Muffins. Don't you worry, the windows are open. We'll check up on you. And later, we'll find a nice spot and watch the fireworks. Okay, little guy?"

He barked.

"I'll take that as a yes."

Holly stood at the top of the hill that led down to the lake. Colorful blankets took up all the spots. Camp chairs, beach chairs galore. Children ran, weaving in between the crowds. Coolers were open. Her desserts would be appealing in this heat. With a smile, she approached a large crowd in the back. Her plan was to find the one in the most need of a break. The hassled husband. The frazzled mom.

This group was large, multiple families. Several coolers. A goldmine waiting to happen. Holly approached from the right, toward the older woman, a grandmother, sitting in a camp chair.

Angry voices greeted her.

"Now is not the time to talk about this." The old woman's voice crackled, strained with effort. "We're here to celebrate."

A man, middle-aged father, polished, good looking, and reeking of pride and money, argued. "There's never a good time, Mother. Some things, like—"

"Anyone want a scrumptious dessert? Nice and cool. Creamy filling. Fresh, chilled fruit."

The man glared at her. Holly shivered at the anger rippling off him.

The woman jumped. "We'd love some. One for everyone."

Within seconds, the many children gathered around Holly, clamoring. She passed them out. The family large enough, Holly gave them half-off.

With an encouraging smile to Ann, who went back to the van for another tray, Holly moved forward. Calling out. She didn't love hand selling, but after much research, felt convicted to go out of her comfort zone. Too much at stake. Her back-up funds wouldn't last forever.

After selling a few more, a blaring voice echoed over the crowd.

"Free cupcakes! A gift from *The Tasty Bite!*"

Holly whipped around. Millicent walked through the crowd with a megaphone, shouting *free cupcakes*. Not only was Millicent stealing Holly's profit, she made *Just Cheesecake* look bad for having people pay. A large felt hat sat on Millicent's head. Blinking red and blue lights were woven into the fabric. All her helpers, local teens, wore the same hat as they passed out free cupcakes.

And Charlene didn't want to wear an apron. Holly deflated as her time and money went down the drain. People turned away, closed their wallets. A quick decision had to be made.

"Free desserts!" Holly called out. She might not have a megaphone, but she had the voice God gave her.

Charlene and Kitty followed suit, and all of a sudden, it turned into a race. Millicent flashed her a wild look and picked up speed, practically throwing the cupcakes at the crowd. When Holly ran out, she raced back to the van for more.

"This is crazy," Charlene huffed. "Maybe we should call it quits. She beat us at our own game. Brilliant though, offering desserts for free. Earning the good will of the people, who then might purchase—" She stopped talking seeing the look on Holly's face.

"I understand the concept of free." Unfortunately, she didn't have the profit yet to offer that many for free. Cupcakes were cheap. Cheesecake tortes with fresh fruit weren't. By losing all this profit, Holly would be down a chunk of change.

She kicked the tire of the van. Tears of frustration brimming, about to fall.

Charlene placed her hand on Holly's arm. "Don't let that girl get to you. If this isn't a smart decision, let's close shop. Recycle the tortes and fresh fruit tomorrow morning. Sell them cheap. Offer them in bundles."

Holly melted. This was the first time in days that Charlene spoke kindly, without a hint of sarcasm. Just more proof something was going on with her. Something she wasn't talking about.

Kitty arrived, panting. "I'm all out. It's a zoo tonight."

They turned just in time to see Millicent's latest stunt. She now was up on stilts, a magnificent and flashy coat draped around her. Several of the teens were now dressed as clowns, red curly hair, painted-on smiles. They handed balloons to people in the crowd.

"Wow." Even though Millicent's tactics were ridiculous and over-the-top, they worked. "Okay, let's stop. Thanks guys. Let's just enjoy the rest of the night."

Charlene hugged her. "Don't worry. We'll figure out a way to top tonight."

"Yeah, sure."

With a nod from Charlene, she and Kitty and Ann melted into the crowds.

Holly locked up the backdoor of the van, not even caring at that point whether the desserts made it through the rest of the night. She opened the driver's door where Muffins waited, barking and impatient. "Let's go, Muffins."

And at the first chance of freedom, Muffins leapt to the ground and took off running.

4

"MUFFINS!" THAT DOG.

He didn't look back once but shot through the crowds, a tiny gray bullet. He leapt coolers, scooted under camp chairs, even snatched a hot dog from a five-year-old's hands.

Exhausted and discouraged from the whole evening, Holly didn't want to chase him. He'd return eventually. But then, as he was about to melt into the darkness, he knocked one of Millicent's cupcakes into the face of an older man ready to take his first bite.

Holly couldn't complain. But she couldn't let the dog run around unleashed. What was she thinking? With a surge of anger and adrenaline that her dog ruined the nice pity party she'd planned, she chased after him.

"Sorry!" she said to the large family who'd been her first customers.

"Excuse me," she shouted to the mom consoling the five-year-old.

She took a second to hand the old man a napkin, frosting smeared across his chin. After receiving a short lecture on dogs and leashes and public places, she stood and searched for the rascal dog.

He was nowhere.

Darkness closed in fast, anticipation growing for the upcoming fireworks display. Kids waved sparklers. Hundreds of glow necklaces and bracelets bobbed back and forth as kids expelled their excitement. Teens attempted to set off their own mini-fireworks, causing a haze of smoke. In the background, Millicent's booming announcement of free cupcakes rattled her.

"Free...aaaaggh!"

A prickly sense of doom fell over Holly. She had a feeling as to why Muffins ran away. Slowly, she turned. Muffins

34

yipped at Millicent's feet, barking and nipping at the ends of the sparkly coat as it whipped in the breeze. A tease. A dog's delight.

Millicent flailed her arms, grasping for something to hold onto that wasn't there. She wobbled one way and lurched forward on her stilts. Her tray of cupcakes flew from her hands into the crowds. Kids dove in mad pursuit. She staggered backward.

Holly cringed, watching with one eye closed. This didn't look good.

Moms and dads grabbed their little ones and pulled them to safety. They scrambled to move their careful spread of food, their soda cans, and their chairs. They yelled and shouted and screamed.

With one last effort, Millicent toppled over, crashing into the parade of clowns who'd been trying desperately to catch their employer.

Holly dashed through, snagged Muffins, and sprinted away.

After Holly found a spot way in the back, in the cool grass, the first fireworks burst into the air with flashing colors and the resounding boom and sparks. The effect was immediate. The crowds calmed and focused on the night sky.

"Bad dog." She snuggled up to Muffins, attempting to hide. Hopefully, Millicent had no idea what caused her spill.

"Mind if I join you?" Trent asked, appearing behind her.

A quick glance told Holly he didn't know anything about Muffins and Millicent and free cupcakes. "Sure. I didn't think to bring a blanket or chair." She thought she'd be selling straight through the evening.

"I have one." He spread a soft beach blanket on the grass.

Holly scooted over onto it. "Thanks."

Another burst sparked the sky, swirly, wiggly flashes of color that then faded out, just for another one to take its place.

"How did your plans go?"

"Fine." It wasn't that Holly didn't want to be truthful, but she couldn't even admit her failed evening to herself, never mind talk about it to anyone. A whole truckload of chilled cheesecake tortes still filled the van. But more than that, she'd been outdone, outmaneuvered, outsmarted by the one person she couldn't stand...or the one person who couldn't stand her.

He chuckled, friendly and warm. "What kind of answer is that? That tells me nothing. Come on, now. My mom has talked about nothing else except for the big plans for tonight."

"Let's say that parts of it worked and parts of it didn't." She blinked back the tears and focused on the sky.

"Oh." He stopped poking and prodding with his questions and settled back, his arm brushing Holly's.

Why did she all of a sudden want the comfort and warmth of a friend? She wanted to snuggle into him and feel his arm around her. It had to be the mood, all the couples and families surrounding her. She missed her parents.

"My first year on the force was tough." Trent cleared his throat, stalling, like this was hard to admit. "I completed more paperwork that year than I care to admit. And when I got an assignment it was for small things, parking tickets, noise disturbances at night, or someone messing with trashcans."

Holly stifled a snicker. "I heard about those exploding trashcans."

He laughed. "Don't even listen to my mom's version. She likes to think she solved the mystery herself. That I couldn't have done it without her."

"I think it's wonderful she likes to help and wants you to succeed. Not everyone has that support from their family."

A lump rose in Holly's throat. "Better than someone trying to sabotage your work."

"You're right. I probably don't tell her enough."

A comfortable silence fell over them. For the first time, in a while, Holly felt connected to Trent. They were friends. And sharing personal stories cemented their friendship. Or whatever it might be as her stomach flip-flopped and her skin tingled at his touch. Maybe this evening could be salvaged from complete disaster.

Fireworks whizzed past them. Holly jumped.

"Whoa. What was that?" Trent wrapped his arm around her and inched closer.

"Those teens over there are fooling around with mini-rockets."

"Kids. I'm off duty, so I'm going to ignore their shenanigans."

Holly couldn't look away though as they tried to light another one. The family who'd purchased her tortes was right near them. The grandmother sat in her chair, nodding off. The parents had their kids tucked in their laps, watching the sky. They were unaware of the danger.

"I don't have a good feeling about this." As much as she wanted to stay in Trent's arms, she stood and walked toward the family. If anything, to warn them about the potential firework hazard just yards away.

It happened lightning fast but slow at the same. Holly saw the firework light. The teens cheered. One knocked the other boy's arm and the rocket bobbled. They had words, shoving each other playfully.

The mini-rocket was aimed at the grandmother.

She started running. "Hey!"

As the rocket exploded, amidst the cheering and booming, Holly tackled the grandmother. Seconds later, the firework whizzed past them.

The grandmother lay limp in her arms. Holly rolled her off, the grandmother's face pale, waxen-looking. She didn't move. She certainly should've startled awake at this point.

"What happened?" one of the sons asked. "She die of fright?"

Holly checked the lady's pulse. Nothing. "Um, possibly?"

"She's dead!" One of the moms screamed. She pointed at Holly. "You killed her!"

HOLLY STARED, AGHAST. Her nightmare of a night just turned deadly. The woman next to her was dead. Just like that. Hadn't she just been sleeping? Or had she looked it, while in reality, she'd slipped from this world into the next? Holly patted the lady's hair, pushing the silver strands out of her face, then she closed the lady's eyes out of respect. Her wrinkled face spoke of years of healthy living, surrounded by her close and loving family.

"Get away from her!" A woman shoved Holly. "You killed her."

Holly scrambled to her feet. What? Didn't anyone notice she'd saved her from a flying rocket? "I didn't kill her."

The woman's face tightened, turned cold and mean. Her bobbed brown hair landed in a point at her chin. Sharp and angled. "So you like to tackle the elderly in your spare time?"

The entire family, shocked, innocent faces, some with tears, turned to stare at her. Small hisses of breath and choked sobs surrounded her. One of her sons was at the grandmother's side, checking her pulse, holding her, rocking her.

Holly stumbled back. "It wasn't like that." She pointed to the huddle of teens but they'd disappeared. Vanished. "There were teens and they had fireworks and they fought..."

"Right. Tell me another one." The lady pulled out her phone and punched at it. Calling the cops.

Holly's feet moved on their own, inching back from the scene, until she bumped into someone.

"What's going on here?" Trent flashed his badge. "Everyone back away." His voice was lost in the grand finale, the last display of brilliance and color.

Except now, the booming and clapping and screaming and whoops were unsettling. Ominous. When the last round faded, the final boom echoed into nothing, the crowds

41

moved. Flashlights turned on, pointed in their direction as the crowds gathered their things to leave, tired but exhilarated.

The lady with short bob pointed a finger at Holly. "She killed my mother-in-law."

That drew everyone's attention. The two sons, probably brothers with the same dark hair and crooked nose, were pale and shocked. The crowd slowed, taking in the scene, listening to the sharp and angry words that accused Holly of deadly intentions. Some stopped and watched. Others ushered their children away.

A light flashed, blinding Holly. When the spots faded, there was Millicent, audio recorder out, interviewing the family. Her stilts were gone, crazy hat gone. Clowns gone.

"I'm so sorry for your loss. What happened?" The smirk on Millicent's face grew, though subtle, as she listened to the report of the evening. Shoddy reporting at best.

Trent took charge. "That's enough. No reporters." He faced the crowds, his voice booming like the fireworks. "This is now a crime scene. Move along, people. Nothing to see."

Sirens sounded in the distance, heading their way. Holly stared at the elderly lady. What had happened?

When Trent enforced the no-reporter rule, Millicent huffed, then headed straight toward Holly. Trent dove into the scene, questioning the family while gently testifying to the grandmother's death.

Holly was on her own.

"Any words?" Millicent asked and clicked Record. "Funny that you always end up right in the middle of it. What do you have to say to that?"

"Um..." The words died before they could be spoken.

"Did you set up your business here specifically with the intent of committing murder?"

Holly stared at Millicent, the light in her eyes, the crooked smile as the rest of the crowd and noise blurred. Murder? She'd tried to save a grandmother from exploding fireworks, but that would never make it into the article. Not Millicent's version.

"Or is that your business plan? Steal sales from competing business by playing dirty."

Playing dirty? Holly awoke from her stupor. She'd show Millicent how to play dirty. Millicent flashed another picture.

"Great one. Thanks!"

Strong hands gripped Holly's arms, pulling her back. She fought. She struggled. She'd tackle Millicent and destroy that no-good camera and audio recorder.

"Whoa, there killer," Charlene whisper-hissed. "Finally, something exciting happened, and I missed it."

"Good thing your little posse is here to prevent your rage from zooming out of control." Millicent smirked. "Have you considered an anger management program? I could help you find one. I'm good at research."

Even though her arms were pinned, Holly's voice finally broke free from the shock. "I bet you are good at spying. Stealing creative designs that can't be patented. Spying and sabotaging my business ideas."

"Pfft. You're just jealous."

"Millicent," Charlene said, "I suggest you don't come to book club this week."

She laughed, almost a cackle. "No problem. I don't need your stupid, ineffective, little detective group to write my novel. I have enough hands-on experience since Heather moved to town."

"That's Holly."

"And, I'll make sure my dad refuses to take orders from any of you. Just wait until you're chatting about your latest whodunit and you don't have my chocolate chip cheesecake."

"Ha!" Charlene roared. "We have a new favorite cheesecake, so good riddance. Yours was always a little heavy on the cream."

Millicent gasped, hurt flickering.

Kitty and Ann arrived, panting and sweaty. "We heard there's a crime scene."

"Oh, lookee. Here's the posse now. Good luck with this one, gals. Looks pretty cut and dried to me. Heather here is a killer."

Trent strode up behind Millicent. "Ladies. You're causing a bigger scene than the crime scene. Break it up."

Millicent huffed. "Have everything I need anyway. But don't worry, Officer Trinket." She traced her fingers down his cheek. "I'll be stopping in bright and early tomorrow morning for your opinion." Then she hurried away, fading into the darkness.

"Now ladies." Trent's scowl deepened. "I suggest you go home. Let the police take care of this. And I mean it this time! Or so help me God I'll put you all in jail."

Charlene straightened, unmoving. "I believe this is a free country, and we can stand here if we like. If you didn't happen to notice the bombs bursting in air."

He growled and turned, but paused and looked back. "I'll stop in later for a statement, Holly. Or I can escort you to the station."

"I'll be home," she whispered. And just like that, the feelings, the warmth, the connection she felt to him, severed. He was back to being cop. She was back to being a suspect, her business and respect on the line.

Muffins growled, then yipped.

"You tell him, Muffins." Holly picked him up.

***

HOLLY PACED IN her small kitchen. She'd fed Muffins and filled his water bowl, and after all the action, he snored on the couch.

The entire night flashed through her mind. Millicent's stunts with the free cupcakes and her crazy marketing scheme. None of that mattered. None of it was important anymore. *Just Cheesecake* would survive being upstaged by the competition. She'd learned valuable lessons—none of which she could focus on.

But would her business survive another murder scandal? Millicent would spout false accusations and lies that would flood the community.

The murder, the grandmother's sweet face, wouldn't leave Holly's memory. The family was crushed, striking out in anger at the nearest target. She couldn't hold that against them.

Worst of all, and she hated herself for this, she couldn't wipe from her mind, Millicent, tracing her fingers against Trent's cheek. It felt like more than a gimmick to gain a cop's attention. It suggested closeness, an intimacy that Holly didn't have with him. What wasn't Charlene telling her?

A knock on the door. "Holly?"

She panicked at the sound of Trent's voice. She patted her hair and smoothed her shirt. Why was she suddenly nervous? She'd done nothing wrong.

"Come in," she said with a cool tone.

Trent entered and sat at the table. He pulled out his notepad, avoiding her gaze. Any feelings he had must've died.

Still focused on the page in front of him, he said, "Would you please share your version of the events?"

After taking a deep breath, Holly dove into the story. She told him about the teens and the fireworks and the nudged arm. She told him about the sleeping grandmother and the distracted family. Then she told him about diving to protect the older lady.

"Did you have any earlier interactions with the family?"

"Well, yes."

Trent's head jerked up, his eyes lacking any warmth. "Explain."

"They were my first customers of the night. She paid for tortes for the whole family. And before you ask, we got along fine. They were nice people."

"I'll be sure to ask them about that. One more question." He closed his notebook and caught her eyes. This time, he allowed her to see his conflict. "Did you have any reason to be angry at Ms. Poppleton?"

Poppleton—she had a name. Holly tucked that information away for later. "Nope." She walked over and opened the door. "If that's all, it's been an exhausting day, and I'd like to go to bed."

He nodded. "I understand." Before leaving, he touched her arm, a soft touch.

Warmth surged through her chest. This could not be happening. She refused to crush on a cop.

"I mean it, Holly. Stay out of this case. We're just starting the investigation, and in no way do I think you had anything to do with the crime, but I'll have to follow procedure." With a sad smile, he left.

Follow procedure. Meaning they couldn't be friends or anything else while she was involved. She trailed her fingers down the door. "Sorry, Trent. But I can't stay out of it."

THE NEXT MORNING, before the crack of dawn, Holly bustled around her apartment. With great surprise, she awoke refreshed, vitalized, and motivated. The day before, her plans, were a big fat failure. She laughed even though it was no laughing matter. What else could she do?

Her competition outplayed her. Beat her at her own game.

Holly decided to let go of the fact that Millicent had stolen her design and passed it along to her father—even though Holly had no idea how she stole it. Pierre, the owner of *The Tasty Bite*, was too nice to steal ideas. If only she could've been a fly on the wall.

She allowed herself one cup of hot coffee with a bit of cocoa mixed in while she read chapters from one of her favorite mystery novels. The paperback was worn, the cover almost falling off. Reading a mystery in one sitting was a thing of the past. Now it was a luxury. Then, she fed Muffins, took him for a short walk with a firm grip on the leash, and made sure he had food and water.

Dressed to work, apron slung over shoulder, she locked her door and headed to *Just Cheesecake*. She thought failure would discourage her and she'd need a pound of chocolate and a night of old mystery movies to feel better. But no, she thought about her family, the reasons she struck out on her own, and a fire sparked. She could do this. And she'd start with selling the rest of the tortes this morning. If it was the last thing she'd do.

First, she parked the refrigerated truck in the front parking lot, easy access to the tortes. Using the rolling cart, she placed as many of the treats as she could on the flat surface and left it in front of her shop, near the front door. Then, she made a huge sign that said free coffee with purchase of torte. She marked the price one dollar. Move the merchandise. Salvage something from the night before. That was the plan.

It worked fast. As soon as she rolled out the cart and taped up the sign and set out the coffee carafes her first customers appeared.

Holly stayed through the morning rush hour wave, people heading to work and craving something sweet and a cup of coffee to get them started. Each customer received a bright smile, a warm hello, and treats to go. With rumors of the murder spreading, the town needed something sweet and some kindness. When that wave dwindled, needing to whip up new batches, she made the decision that the town was trustworthy and she left everything as is with a bowl to drop cash. She headed back to the kitchen.

In the next couple hours, only stopping to refill the carafe and bring out more tortes, she mixed cheesecake to store in the freezer. Then she popped cheesecakes in the oven. Oreo, chocolate chip, strawberry, and cherry. These staples sold the best.

While getting lost in what she loved to do, she also brainstormed marketing ideas. Ways to get her cheesecake out there, recognized. New creations. Special deals. Free deliveries. And lots of hard work.

She barely even thought about the night before.

The morning hours flew by. Finally, she heard the bell above the door. She rushed out to the front room and found Charlene.

"Why didn't you call me? You were going to take today off."

Holly wiped a smudge of cheesecake from her nose. "I woke up inspired."

"I refilled the cart for you." Charlene glanced around the place. "Where's all the customers?"

Holly had been so busy baking and brainstorming, she hadn't realized that what started out as a great day of business had fizzled out. Not many customers had entered the shop. The daily paper was tucked under Charlene's arm.

"Let me guess." Holly pointed to the paper. "Another flattering article about me by Millicent, the star reporter."

Charlene ignored her comment. "If you're done, I say you close early. I've called an emergency meeting of the mystery club. I told the ladies to meet here at noon. Exactly thirty minutes."

They worked in silence, storing in the fridge the remaining tortes, many of which had sold. They washed and cleaned the carafes and left them on the side table in the front room. Just about that time, Kitty and Ann showed up.

"Alright, we're all here." She nodded toward the kitchen. "Can we meet back there?"

"Um, sure." Holly wondered why the secrecy, why the note of determination. Now she really wanted to read that article. There were so many different and negative spins— more like outright lies—that Millicent could put on what happened.

They gathered in the kitchen, standing in a huddle, and Charlene spoke first. "I took it upon myself to invite Trent over for breakfast this morning. He never could refuse bacon."

"Isn't that obvious?" Holly asked. "He had to have seen right through that scheme to subtly interrogate him about the murder."

Charlene's mouth dropped open and she forced out a fake gasp. "He is my son. Our meals together keep me going."

"That, and solving mysteries." Kitty chuckled.

"And that. But make no mistake. There was nothing subtle about breakfast this morning. I asked outright what he knew so far."

"And?" Holly, Kitty, and Ann said at the same time.

"He told me to stay out of it."

The ladies laughed. Of course, Holly thought. Trent was smart. The minute Charlene asked him to breakfast, he knew she wanted information.

"And then..." Everyone snapped to attention, the laughter ceasing. "He told me the victim was Agatha Poppleton."

Kitty and Ann murmured. Charlene looked smug.

Holly didn't understand why that was such a big deal. "Even I knew that."

"Okay, miss smarty pants." Charlene narrowed her eyes. "Tell me then why that name is so significant."

"Well...she was older...lots of grand children. Definitely an undercurrent of tension last night. I'd say it could be a family squabble."

"Ha!" Kitty blurted. "I told you she'd be a good addition to our club."

Charlene waved her away. "Nonsense. Anyone with any sense of observation could've figured that out. She's no Sherlock."

"Fine, then. Tell me what I missed," Holly said. "Please remember I've only been in town for a few months."

Ann spoke quietly. "A few years ago there was a huge dispute with the Poppleton family. Many say the children were trying steal their mother's home. Put her away in a retirement center." She pursed her lips. "I can't remember the details."

Charlene slammed her fist into the palm of her other hand. "Time for some investigative work, ladies. This murder isn't going to solve itself. Trent's waiting for the lab results and following up with interrogation today. He can't do much without knowing cause of death. The old lady could've had a heart attack for all we know."

"I can check the town newspaper from the last few years." Ann cracked her fingers, ready for an afternoon in the library. "It shouldn't be too hard to track down."

Kitty talked before Charlene could give the order. "I'll check at the town offices for any leads regarding their properties."

"Sounds like a plan." Charlene placed her hand in the center. Kitty and Ann followed suit, like they were part of a basketball team.

Tentatively, Holly placed her hand on top. What would her job be? Instinct told her Charlene was saving that for last. So why did she feel like she was back in elementary school?

"On three, ladies," Charlene said.

"Wait! What are we saying?" Holly asked.

"Go! Go! Murder club! Now, on three." Charlene counted down and they all shouted the cheer.

Kitty and Ann left for their tasks, leaving Charlene and Holly. The air crackled with unspoken tension as Charlene studied Holly.

"What?" Holly busied herself in the kitchen, uncomfortable under the stare. "What can I do?"

"You had a point earlier. Trent expects me to question him, especially the day after a murder. He probably had his pat answers prepared before he arrived at my house."

"Probably. He's a smart man."

Charlene grinned. "And handsome, too. Right?"

A blush stole across Holly's cheeks. There might've been something, but this murder investigation put a damper on any sparks.

"I knew it!" Charlene laughed.

"Oh, you don't know anything. What do you want me to do?"

"Use your youthfulness to keep Trent distracted for the afternoon while I sneak into his office and poke around. Maybe find the lab results."

"My youthfulness?" Holly asked, doubtful.

"You know…" Charlene waved. "Bat your eyes. Smile. Act needy. He's a sucker for things like that."

"Shame on you," Holly said. "You want me to trick your son, using my feminine charms, into giving me information."

"Exactly. Bingo. She's finally got it." Charlene pulled out the folded town paper. "But it has to happen naturally. You storm into *The Tasty Bite*, cause a scene, rant and rave at Pierre. I'll send Trent after you. Trust me. He'll never suspect a thing."

"But I'm not mad at him. And this morning, I took responsibility for last night. What I thought was a great idea, Millicent blew out of the water."

Charlene held out the paper. "Then read this."

FLASH! BANG! BOOM!

The Tasty Bite **takes all on the Fourth!**

Pierre Monroe and The Tasty Bite have done it again. His ingenious ideas were as explosive as the fireworks lighting up the sky. While cozy couples, happy families, and children galore enjoyed the benefits of a small community celebrating our great country, Pierre delighted one and all with his generous donation of free holiday cupcakes.

That's right. Free.

He has spent years building up the trust and loyalty of this town. Other businesses come and go, but you can always depend on The Tasty Bite.

His yummy treats brought smiles to faces and delight to the taste buds. He thought of his customers first with clowns, balloons, and smiles. What a horror to think others might charge and steal money from your pockets. Don't you worry; Pierre's got you covered.

Visit The Tasty Bite for your free holiday cupcake today!

THEY HAD TIMED their watches down to the last second. In exactly twenty minutes, Charlene would call Trent, scared out of her mind because Holly had finally lost her cool. She'd beg Trent to go to *The Tasty Bite* and intercept Holly before she took her anger out on Pierre.

Except, Holly didn't feel one ounce of rage at Pierre. She didn't want to yell at him or cause a scene. That would make her and *Just Cheesecake* look bad. Like sore losers. Which she wasn't.

Charlene said she had to be willing to make that sacrifice, and then later, they'd pitch in and do whatever Holly asked of them when it came to selling cheesecake.

That could be fun. She laughed out loud, picturing Charlene in a ridiculous outfit. She cleared her throat, containing her glee. She was supposed to be furious, out of her mind with rage. Millicent's articles almost always put a negative slant on *Just Cheesecake*, without even mentioning the name. She played dirty. That was enough to make her mad. But she also thought it was sweet that Millicent went to any length to help her dad.

Instead of anger, sadness swept through Holly. She'd wasted her teenage years mad at her parents for their rules and restrictions. Now she'd give anything to sit down to dinner and chat with them. Talk about her thoughts and feelings. Had she ever given them that chance? Not really.

The Tasty Bite came into view. Again, the place was packed, customers coming and going, hands full of sweet desserts. She closed her eyes and tried to summon the anger she felt when reading the article, when seeing Millicent trounce around with her free cupcakes.

"Oh, Trent. Thank you so much." Millicent's words dripped with sugary seduction.

The recognizable voice came from behind her. Holly dove into bushes that lined the road. She had a few minutes before Charlene would call Trent, but he was already here. Her legs cramped in the crouched position, but Holly ignored the pain and peeked over the bush.

What?

Millicent leaned on crutches, her ankle wrapped in about five layers of supportive tape. "They never tell you how sore your hands get using these things."

Holly fumed. Why were they walking down the sidewalk, like friends...or lovers?

"Maybe you should be resting at home or the newspaper office. Going through old files or something like that." He scratched his head and looked down the road as if needing an out.

She hobbled past and glanced at the bushes. Had she seen Holly?

"Oh, please. Trenty-poo. Could we stop and rest for a second?"

Trenty-poo? Holly wanted to gag and roll over on the spot.

"Sure." He helped her over to the bench right in front of Holly, then he sat next to her. "How did you hurt your foot?

You were dashing around last night just fine. Nosing in crime scenes, as usual."

Millicent giggled, high and flirty. "I was just doing my job. You can understand that. We're both in the line of real investigation, unlike other amateurs in this town."

"Real investigation?" He sounded doubtful.

"You're a cop. I'm an investigative reporter." Millicent made it sound like the connection between the two jobs should be obvious. "I completely understand the frustration when dealing with the general public and their interference, and sometimes backlash, in our professional work."

Trent didn't respond. Holly silently cheered. He might not like when she landed smack in the middle of a murder investigation, but obviously, he couldn't agree with Millicent's outlandish comparison.

He chuckled. "There definitely is interference and backlash. I know exactly what you mean."

What? Holly wanted to slug him. Now she was angry.

Millicent draped her arm over his lap. "For example, last night. I was offering my valuable time to my dad, helping him with his business, especially with everything going on—"

"That's right. How is your father doing?"

"He's managing." Millicent fell silent. "The arthritis gets to him. That's why I help whenever I can. It's hard managing two jobs, but I'd do anything for him." She lifted her arm and smoothed his hair away from his face in a loving gesture, one that suggested intimacy. "That's why I'm so thankful for friends like you. Not sure how I would make it otherwise."

"Any time, Millicent. Now what happened to that ankle? Maybe you should see a doctor."

"Well, I don't like to talk about it." She raised her voice. "Someone—I don't want to mention names because that's not very nice—had their dog attack me when I was up on stilts. It was horrible. When I fell, I twisted my ankle."

Trent's phone buzzed. "Hold on a second." He answered it. "Hello, Trent here...Can't talk now, Mom...No, really...I'll call you back." Then he hung up.

Holly glanced at her watch. That was the call. Trent was supposed to be off saving Holly from making a mistake, but he was so wrapped up in Millicent's charm that he brushed off his mom!

As soon as he was off the phone, Millicent continued, "Can you believe it? There I was, offering free cupcakes, giving back to the community, and someone couldn't handle the competition. It was just awful."

Holly detected the hint of a sob in Millicent's voice. If only Muffins were with her, then she'd tell her big, ferocious dog to attack.

"We need to be careful about newcomers to town." She wrapped her finger in his hair. "Do you think we should do a little investigative work? Especially when one has been directly involved in so many murders?"

Trent straightened. "Why don't you leave that to the police? Anyone's free to come and go in this town, without providing their life story."

"Well, I was just saying." She cheered up. "I've got a great idea. Why don't you help me over to *The Tasty Bite*? We'll get one of those free cupcakes. I've been meaning to talk to you."

Trent's phone buzzed again, and he ignored it. There went their plan. Obviously, Charlene didn't need Holly to distract Trent. Millicent had that well under control. As she watched them trot off to *The Tasty Bite*, Millicent taking advantage of Trent's closeness as often as possible, Holly tried to ignore the surge of jealousy. Something happened between her and Trent the other night. But then why was he kissing up to Millicent today?

She should go home. Bake cookies. Eat all of them. And watch a movie. Instead, she followed Millicent and Trent into *The Tasty Bite*. What did she need to talk to Trent about? Did she have information on the Poppletons?

Holly had no choice but to do a little investigating. Instead of sneaking around though, she'd go with a different approach. Just be herself. Melt into the crowds invading *The Tasty Bite*.

At the door, Holly entered behind a family of five. She managed to stay out of Millicent and Trent's sight by maneuvering her position. Something else bothered Holly. Mixed in with all the lies, Millicent had mentioned she helped her dad because he was in pain. That information tugged on Holly's heart. She peeked at Pierre, smiling, laughing, engaging with his customers. How could she ever have faked a fight?

Instead, she sat at tiny table in the corner. It was too noisy to hear anything, so she waited. Customers came and went, and thankfully, Millicent had Trent so wrapped up in conversation that they didn't notice her.

After a while, the crowds dissipated, and a quiet hush fell over the place.

"Why look who's here!" Millicent called. "Checking out the competition, Heather? I don't blame you. Not after last night."

Holly was about to give a sassy reply when the phone rang behind the counter. She listened as Pierre took what appeared to be a large order.

"A party for thirty? In two days? This is kind of last minute...yes...I see...I'm sure I can manage...okay, thank you." Then, Pierre disappeared into the kitchen, the order pad with the address left on the counter. An idea sparked.

She turned, offering a sweet smile. "I didn't get a chance to taste one of the holiday cupcakes. Especially after noticing the magnificent design on the Fourth of July special edition cake." Holly pointed to the front table where the cake sat on display. "Look at the bright colors, the use of different kinds of cakes. Ingenious. Really." As she spoke, Holly inched closer to the notepad. "Your father must have spent hours creating that design."

Millicent shifted, uncomfortable, her cheeks pink. Good to know she had a conscience. Obviously, not a big one.

Turning her back to them, Holly pretended to study the glass showcase, but instead memorized the address on the notepad.

188 Hilltop Drive.

"My father will be out in a second. He'd be happy to take your order."

Holly couldn't take the fakery. "Thanks, but I need to be going. I'm so sorry about your ankle. I hear stilts can be pretty dangerous. I'll leave you two on your date."

After one last look at Trent's face, which lacked any kind of expression, Holly left. Instead of storming *The Tasty Bite*, she stormed down the street. She sent a text to Charlene then shut off her phone.

Trent will be distracted for a while. You're all set.

This whole day had been a roller coaster. Up and down. Up and down. After stopping at home to check on Muffins, she'd have to meander out to Hilltop Drive.

THE WORDS WERE burned into her brain. Hilltop Drive. Her chance at revenge. Even if Pierre was ignorant to the whole thing, *The Tasty Bite* had stolen her design for the Fourth of July cake. She would not and could not hold their ingenious planning against them the night of the fireworks. They killed it.

Muffins curled up on her lap, snoozing. Holly stroked his back, absently thinking about getting off the couch and driving out to Hilltop. She'd knock on the door and let the owners know of her fabulous half-off deal. After all, Pierre sounded distracted on the phone, like he barely had time to squeeze in this new order. She'd be helping him out. Right?

"Holly?" Trent knocked on the door.

Holly didn't move. She was upset with him but didn't have the right. Was she the only one who felt their connection? Then today he fell for Millicent's charm without blinking an eye.

"Yes?" She knew he wouldn't leave her alone.

"I have a warrant to search your apartment and your shop. Open up."

What? Holly glanced around frantically. She thought of the scattered clothes on her bedroom floor, the pile of dirty laundry. The dishes in the sink. She gently moved Muffins off her lap.

"What do you mean—a warrant?" Of course, she knew exactly what he meant.

"It's protocol. The autopsy confirmed poison."

"What?" She leapt up and opened the door.

Trent stood with a couple of officers behind him. His expression was grim, his gaze peering past her into her home. "That's right. Arsenic. Probably administered a little bit here and there over time." He pushed past her into her apartment. "We have to check out any named suspect. The

Poppleton family named you. Just following through. I'm sure you understand."

"Oh, definitely. I wouldn't want to hold back a murder investigation." She turned to the officers. "Don't mind the hot pink lace panties on the bedroom floor. I wasn't expecting company."

With a grimace—or was it gleam of excitement?—they started the search. Trent leaned against the door, casual, unhurried, one leg crossed over the other, hands in his pocket. He looked over the living room and the kitchen, lazily soaking everything in.

"You don't seem too convinced of my guilt." She thought about the words that Millicent had planted in Trent's mind. Casting doubt on Holly and her past. Hopefully, he meant what he said about people having a right to their privacy when it came to their past.

"Oh, I'm not." He smiled, a wicked grin. "Or maybe it's an act. My plan to lull you into trusting me."

"Why would you inform me of that?" Holly attempted to strike a casual pose, prove that none of this bothered her.

"You'll never know, I guess. You'll have to trust me. I know I'm an officer of the law, untrustworthy until proven loyal and true in all situations. I remember, Holly Hart."

"I don't think you're dirty," she said, and she meant it. Didn't mean she was ready to throw her heart and secrets at him though.

He pushed off the door and sauntered into the kitchen, examining, studying. "Maybe not. But you don't trust me."

How could she? He gallivanted about with Millicent Monroe, listening to her like she was a visiting preacher with authority straight from God.

"That's right. I see it in your eyes." He opened cupboards and poked through her cooking supplies.

"Don't forget the pantry. You might want to test the vegetable oil. I might have disguised the poison."

"Good idea."

Muffins woke and yipped. She glanced at him. I know, I know she tried to communicate silently. I should be following Charlene's plan. Flirting. Talking. Pulling Trent off guard to distract and gain information. Any time she opened her mouth to giggle or make a light comment, she couldn't do it. Not after seeing him with Millicent. Not after seeing him fall prey to her madness and seduction and fakery. Not after the connection Holly had made with him at the fireworks.

72

"So, poison, huh?" Way to go, Holly, she mocked herself. Way to flirt.

"Yup." He closed the last cupboard. "Nice bit of arsenic."

"How awful. And I thought she was sleeping. Anything else you can tell me?"

He pulled out a kitchen chair and sat. "I guess I owe you that much. If I barge into your home and pick through your unmentionables, I should explain. Sounds fair."

The officers returned from the scavenger hunt. "All clear, sir."

Trent nodded. "Alright, then. Continue with your work. Head to her shop. I'll catch up later."

With a huff, Holly handed over the key, knowing they wouldn't find a thing.

When the officers left, the apartment felt smaller, the space between her and Trent narrowed. She tried not to notice his good looks, his mouth, or his hair. Focus! What would Charlene say right about now? Holly almost laughed. Charlene would encourage her.

"Sorry about the invasion of privacy. So what do you want to know?"

"Who are the main suspects as of now? Other than me," she added.

"We're mainly looking at the Poppleton family. Where there's money, and lots of it, there's motive. We're looking into the children, their finances, their backgrounds. Who might benefit from receiving an early inheritance."

"Anything specific about them?" Holly thought about Ann researching at the library. The Poppletons had made news before.

"Nothing concrete at this point. How about you?"

"What?"

"Did you notice anything the night of the fireworks. Anything unusual? Something that didn't make sense until after."

Holly thought back to when she first approached the family. At the time, she'd felt jealous at the large number of them, siblings, cousins, and grandchildren. She had none of that any more. "Underneath the family picnic mode of happiness there was a current of tension. Nothing I can pinpoint. I already told you everything."

"You're right. Sometimes we remember details later."

Their conversation dwindled. Charlene needed more time. "What's next in the investigation?"

"Like I said,"—he appeared amused—"we'll go on and investigate the Poppletons."

Awkward silence enveloped them. She tried to muster up the courage to say something flirtatious, but it didn't feel right. He'd know it too. Yes, they'd had a moment of connection at the fireworks, but the romantic feelings could've been all on her part. Not his. Especially after she'd brought up his mom dating again, and he'd adamantly refused to discuss it.

He shifted in the chair, fidgeting. Finally, he said, "I've been meaning to talk to you. I've been thinking about what you said about my mom."

"Really?"

He coughed. "You might have a point. She could be lonely."

Holly leaned back, amazed. She never thought he'd be open to it. "What made you change your mind?"

"Time. Thinking back on the past year."

Holly tapped her fingers against the table, unable to contain her enthusiasm. "Your mom has such a great heart under that tough exterior. Your dad must've been a wonderful man, and I can tell she misses him. I'm not even sure who's available to date. What does she like to do? Any hobbies?"

Trent studied his hands, a little too intently. Was he having second thoughts?

"It's not like she'd get married next week. Maybe she needs companionship, male companionship. Someone her age. Who also likes mysteries or puzzles. Someone to take walks with. That sort of thing. She's been such a good friend to me, since the first day I moved to town, welcoming me in her own way. I'd do anything to help her like she's encouraged me."

He slammed his hand on the table. "Stop it." He stood, his chair jerking back, almost falling over. He paced, glancing over at her every once in a while. After a deep breath, he sat back down. "I can't do it. I'm sorry."

"What do you mean?" Holly asked.

"I can't have this conversation with you without telling you the whole truth. That's just not the kind of man I am."

HOLLY DIDN'T WANT to know this truth Trent referenced. Her heart sank. Was it concerning Millicent? Or the murder?

"What is it?" she asked softly, fighting the sadness welling up inside her that her suspicions about cops were right all along. Couldn't trust them.

"I know everything. I know my mom is at my office right now, rifling through my folders, looking for new information. I knew she sent you to cause a scene at *The Tasty Bite* as soon as she called me on the phone with her concerns. It's a complete set-up. Both of you playing me like I'm a piano."

He stood, trembling. "But you couldn't do it. You couldn't yell at the kindest man in town. So here you are, probably under orders to distract me, give my mom more time—and I was willing to play that game. Rehash case information. Talk specifics that's not too sensitive."

When he said it like that, their plans sounded horrible and unfair. Sneaky and deceptive. "I'm sorry. I know you're trying to do your job, and we're interfering." Not that she was all that sorry about that. "I've accused you of not being honest, and here I am scheming with your mom, distracting you from your job. I don't blame you for being upset."

"I expect that of my mom and her friends. You included. Like I said, I've been one step ahead the whole time. That doesn't bother me. But I can't have this kind of personal conversation about my mom while we're playing this game. I can't do it. Not when I know you care about her." He paused, pursing his lips. "But I will have that conversation another time, after I play my cards. I know she's not going to stop sleuthing, so I leave crumbs, drop hints. I keep her distracted while I do the real work."

Holly's thoughts swirled. He was playing a game? What exactly did that mean?

"Let me explain. I'm sitting here, talking with you, distracting you. My mom is poking around at the office. My men are now free to do their detective work without anyone following them or interfering." His eyes softened, regretful. "I play Millicent's games. Keep her happy so she doesn't interfere, so she stays on my side. Unfortunately, her paper can do some damage. I don't want my relationship with you, our friendship, to be based on games."

He knew everything? And they thought they were fooling him. Her respect and admiration for Trent jumped about one hundred points. He was sexy cute and smart. A hint of a smile crept onto her face.

His phone beeped. Holly pretended not to listen as he talked.

"Yes...I'm wrapping it up here...really?...I've got the papers with me. They can't argue with that...be right there." He stood. "And no, I'm not telling you where I'm off to."

He was at the door when Holly blurted, "What about Millicent and all your flirting this afternoon?"

Trent smiled, a seductive, charming grin that caused her heart to beat faster. "Why Holly Hart. I do believe you're jealous."

She stuttered out explanations and arguments. "Pfft. Well...I wouldn't say that...you're allowed to flirt with anyone you'd like."

He strode over and pulled Holly to her feet. She felt unsteady, off balance, so close to him. She heard his soft breathing, smelled his aftershave, close, intimate.

"There's only one girl I want." Slowly, he leaned down and placed a soft, gentle kiss on her mouth. When he pulled away, Holly's legs felt ready to buckle underneath her. "But I'm not going to play games. Not with you."

Then he left the apartment.

***

HOLLY GRIPPED THE steering wheel, Muffins on the seat next to her. His puppy-dog eyes seemed to accuse her.

"Oh, don't you dare give me that look. It was one little kiss." One little kiss. That was it.

Muffins turned away and peered out the window.

"You're a watchdog and not a very good one at that lately considering how often you've run away since moving here. You are not my mother, judging who I should kiss or not kiss." Why was she talking to her dog? Obviously, he didn't care whom she dated. Or maybe he was warning her off dating cops?

She shook it off and focused on following directions to Hilltop Drive. She didn't like deceiving Pierre, stealing his large order, but this wasn't about Pierre. It was about Millicent.

The drive to the outskirts of town was gorgeous. The various plants and bushes flowered in beautiful colors. The oak and maple trees towered over yards, offering shade. Paved roads turned to dirt, twisting and winding. Holly couldn't believe the gorgeous homes, hidden out here, tucked away from the curious eyes of tourists.

It wasn't hard to find 188 Hilltop Drive.

The rambling farmhouse sat back off the road. It was painted a classic white, the lawns meticulously manicured. Holly guessed a couple lived there with lots of money to pay landscapers to work on their house every week or an older couple who loved their home, puttering about, tending to it every day.

"Muffins, stay here. I'll be right back." She cracked the window for him.

After Trent had left earlier, Holly had gathered her supplies: an assortment of her cheesecake tortes, minis, and cakes. She pulled together her business cards and brochure of offerings. Hopefully, the combination of her delectable desserts and half-off sale would cement this deal.

Leaving the guilt behind, she knocked on the front door. When no one answered she was not to be deterred. The warm day was perfect for sitting outside. She'd roam innocently to the backyard.

"Hello?" she called, standing at the edge of the backyard.

The place bloomed with a flower garden, filled with wild flowers of every color. A stretch of yard with the greenest grass she'd ever seen led to a stone wall edging the trees. The wall lined the entire yard, wrapping around to the side. She followed it with her eyes until it stopped right next to her. Except, this part, the stone wall had collapsed, large stones scattered as if they were child's toys. The run-down appearance didn't fit with the rest of the property.

"Who's there?"

Holly straightened and walked with confidence into the backyard toward the voice. An older woman, with long silver hair, sat in a wicker chair set on a stone patio. A ball of yarn lay in a basket at her feet, and her needles clicked furiously.

"Hello there. My name is Holly Hart." She paused. Maybe she should've left out her name after all the disparaging articles Millicent had penned about her.

"Holly Hart. I'm Andrea Givingsworth. What are you selling? I know you've got to be selling something. No one ever visits."

"The most delicious desserts you've ever tasted." Without being invited, Holly approached the lady and set her tray of desserts in front of her. "I'm the owner of a new cheesecake shop in town, *Just Cheesecake*. To get word out about my fantastic cakes, I'm running a special half-off deal for a limited time. High quality cakes for a fraction of the cost."

Andrea didn't say anything, studying Holly, her needles never stopping.

Holly didn't want to ramble, but she couldn't stand the awkward silence. "I don't normally go door-to-door but thought the best way to spread word about my shop was to offer a deal at this holiday time."

"What kind of deal?"

With a sigh of relief that the lady seemed interested, Holly said, "Half-off a custom order for parties or small gatherings." Holly nudged the tray closer to the lady, waiting. "Gorgeous home you have here. I can tell you spend a lot of time on it."

"Thank you. Thomas and I have put a lot of time and money into our property." She glanced at the broken-down stone wall and a frown creased her face. "Half-off, you say?"

"Yes. Tell me when and how much, and I'll have it here. Half down now, and you can pay the other half after I deliver."

Andrea reached a wrinkled hand out and picked up one of the mini-cheesecakes. She took a small bite. Seconds later, a smile spread across her face, and Holly knew she'd scored.

"You've got yourself a deal, Holly Hart. I'll let you decide which treats to bring. We'll be having thirty guests. In two days. Is that enough notice?"

"Yes, I can do it. No problem." Holly expected a busy night of baking. She worked out the details with Andrea and tucked the check into her back pocket. "Thank you. I appreciate your willingness to invest and support a new company in town." Holly placed her business card next to the tray, then took a chance. "Do you know of any other neighbors or friends who might be interested in receiving information on my company?"

"Neighbors?" Andrea asked. She was about to answer when footsteps scraped the patio behind them.

A man, who seemed a lot older than Andrea, stopped next to them, shovel in hand, work clothes rumpled and dirty. Thinning white hair crowned his head. "We have neighbors, but you won't want to be bothering them."

"Oh, yes, that's true." Andrea leaned forward. "I hear it's murder."

Murder? Holly perked up. That could only mean one murder. "I think I heard something about that. Too bad. An older woman passed away in the midst of her family."

Andrea huffed. "I suppose so." She glanced left and right. "I hear her grandchildren are fighting for the money, their inheritance."

"Andrea, that's enough." Thomas's voice turned sharp.

"Why don't you go back to work on that wall!" she snapped.

"Yes, dear." Then he shuffled away.

Holly sensed a brooding fight. That behind the few words they spoke to each other lay a sensitive topic. Time for her to leave. "Again, thank you for your time. I'll see you in a couple days."

Holly escaped back to the front. Perhaps she could stop by, innocently, at the Poppletons, and offer her condolences.

THE POPPLETONS HAD money in the family. That much was quite clear. The three-story house—if you could call it that and not refer to it as a mansion—stretched across the entire property. A sunroom here. An addition there. A four-car garage. Money is always a motive when it comes to murder. Greed and need start small, and then slowly build, a fire, finally consuming a person. Until...

She shook off those thoughts. This family was innocent until proven guilty. They were in mourning, the loss of a matriarch rippling through the family like a cold chill that can't be shaken.

"I'll be right back, Muffins." She rubbed his head. "You're being so patient. I promise. This is the last stop. Extra treats tonight."

He whimpered.

"Sorry, boy. Can't have you running like crazy in the house."

She picked up her business card and the tray of samplers. Instead of offering the half-off deal, she'd leave the treats as her way of helping out, offering condolences.

At the front step, she hesitated. This family had named her as a possible suspect, because she'd tried to save Agatha from a stray firework. Or maybe because they were looking to cast suspicion away from them. Her hand raised, she paused again, listening. Not a sound came from the other side. A somber feel leaked past the door.

She knocked before she could change her mind.

Holly thought back on the night of the murder. The pale, shocked faces of the two men, the cold, angry accusations of the woman. Hopefully, one of the men, probably sons, would open the door, and there would be lots of the grandchildren around to distract, to cover the awkward silence, to gobble up her treats.

She knocked again. If no one came this time, she'd leave. Return later. Maybe with Charlene. Someone to act as a buffer.

The house stayed silent, so Holly turned, almost relieved. The draft hit her legs before she heard the creak of the opening door. With a breath, she turned again.

A child stood in the doorway. About ten years old. Dark hair, the flawless skin of youth, yet her face was pale, like she'd been indoors since the night of the murder. She sucked on a lollipop.

"Hi there. What's your name?" Holly asked. She tried to peer past the girl into the home.

"Cassie." The girl eyed the tray of treats.

"I'm Holly. Are your parents home?" She held out the tray. "Would you like one?"

The girl reached for one, choosing a mini-cheesecake, one of Holly's favorites. A hand snaked in out of nowhere and grabbed Cassie's wrist before she could take a bite.

"Go to your room, Cassie."

Holly had been hoping for one of the sons, not the lady with the brown bob who was all sharp angles and hard words. She was the one who accused Holly of murder.

A few words stuttered out before Holly managed to say, "I wanted to offer my condolences for your loss."

"Thank you." The woman wouldn't budge from the door, no sign of welcoming Holly inside.

"I thought you might enjoy these treats. If you could show me to the kitchen I'll just drop the tray off and be on my way."

With cold disdain, the woman said, "Follow me."

Holly searched the rooms for anything, not that she expected to see a bottle labeled arsenic lying on a coffee table. No, this mission had to be more about gathering information, hoping for a slip-up. The woman's heels clicked against the wood floor. She walked with small but determined steps. There wouldn't be any slip-ups from her.

They entered a large, family kitchen. From the outside of the house, Holly expected granite countertops, stainless steel appliances, and perfection. What she walked into was a well-worn kitchen that hadn't been updated in at least a quarter of a century. A long oak table with seats for twelve stretched along one side. Holly loved the room. It felt cozy, cheerful, the place everyone would congregate in the morning for coffee and breakfast.

Holly placed the tray on the table. "Compliments of *Just Cheesecake*. We're the new—"

"You've got guts." The woman turned fast, catching Holly off guard. "I remember you from the other night. Tackling my mother-in-law. Killing her."

Holly stuck out her hand. "My name's Holly. I'm afraid we got off on the wrong foot."

The lady turned away, stared out the window. After a few seconds, she sniffled.

"I truly am sorry for your loss." Holly inched away from the kitchen, her feet sliding across the floor. Clearly this was a bad idea. She should never have thought subtly interrogating this family was smart.

When Holly was at the entrance to the kitchen, the woman said, "I'm curious." She faced Holly again, her eyes narrowed, her body rigid with tension. "Why would you come?"

Holly thought of a million excuses that would sound good but ring false. She sighed and went with the partial truth. "I miss my family. When I was in the midst of your large one, it reminded me of mine. I connected for that moment. I know I don't know any of you, but I truly am sorry for your loss."

The woman softened. "Oh."

Footsteps thundered on the steps moments before one of the dark-haired sons entered the room. "Oh, no. Driving away guests?" He bustled about the kitchen in a constant state of movement. "Don't let the wicked witch of the west here scare you off. She's more bark than she is bite." He winked and held out his hand. "I'm Donovan. Welcome." He pointed to the woman. "This is Clara."

Clara sniffed. "I was getting to introductions."

"Sure," Donovan said. "I bet you were."

"I'm Holly." She pointed to the tray. "Just dropped by to provide some treats during this tough time." She had to muster up some courage. The whole reason she came here was to find clues. "Sorry to hear about the verdict of murder. I'm sure it's been hard having the police poke around, asking questions."

Donovan waved her off. "They're doing their job. It's expected. We pointed them right away to the old hag next door. She's been greedy for this property for years. Probably finally lost her senses, blinded by years of fantasizing."

"Andrea?" Holly bit her lip as soon as she said the name.

Clara jerked her head. "You know her."

"Not that well, no. I'll be honest. I'm providing desserts for a party."

Donovan jumped up to sit on the counter. "See what I mean? The hag has no decency. Probably throwing a party to celebrate our loss, thinking we might sell."

The other brother entered, bringing with him a cold silence. Donovan lost his enthusiasm. "What're you babbling on about now?" He glared at Holly. "And with a stranger. Stop running your mouth."

Donovan flashed Holly a smile. "Meet Derek, my older brother. And yes, he really is this gloomy all the time."

Derek turned his glare onto his brother. "Someone needs to look after the family. Especially now. Why'd you let her inside?"

"I was curious," Clara stated. "She's the one who tackled Mother at the fireworks."

Holly took small steps, the impending storm, the tension, crackled in the room.

Donovan laughed. "You heard the cop. She died of poison. Anyway, I saw the whole thing. Those boys fooling around with the rockets."

"Exactly!" Holly said. At least she had one witness to back up her story.

"Why are you here?" Derek stepped closer, his dark eyes set off his growing temper.

"J-just to drop off the cheesecakes. Something for the little ones. And for the adults."

"Right." Each step Derek took toward her, Holly took one back, closer to the door. "Somehow I don't believe you. I know your type. Nosing around here, hunting for information. Wanting to clear your name. Probably thinking one of us offed her for the money. Our big inheritance."

Relief surged through Holly when she backed into the front door. She wasn't about to tell Derek that's exactly what she thought. "Again, terribly sorry for your loss. Enjoy the cheesecake." She whipped open the door and stumbled down the steps.

"Right. You're probably to kill all of us off with poison in the cheesecake!" Derek slammed the door.

On the verge of tears, all her confidence drained, she tripped on her way to the car. After picking herself up, she climbed inside, shaking. A brief look in the rearview mirror showed a police cruiser parking behind her. Trent sat at the wheel.

Holly took off, leaving behind a cloud of dust as her wheels spun out. Seconds later, the sirens wailed and the flashing lights reflected.

11

HOLLY STEPPED ON it, her clunky car revving beneath her, the engine vibrating up through her legs. The siren wailed, commanding her to pull over. She pushed her car to go faster, flying down the dirt roads. Adrenaline rushed.

Trent stated he didn't want to play games. His actions said otherwise. She did absolutely nothing wrong by stopping at the Poppletons for a friendly visit. Where was Millicent now with her flashing camera and sarcastic wit?

The light flashing behind her, Holly sped forward. She jumped ahead to the possible outcomes. She'd seen too many car chases in movies and TV shows to know the outcome was never positive. She imagined flipping over, her car bursting into flames. She slowed and pulled over. Furious. Scared. Shaky.

She rolled down her window, ready to strike. The blue uniform appeared beside her. "I know, I know," she said, not attempting to hide the sarcasm. "Speeding, right? Save it for the judge."

"Ma'am, step out of the car, please."

A feeling of dread passed through her. Her scalp tingled. That wasn't Trent's voice. She peered at a female cop, black hair stretched tight into a bun behind her head, hat pushed forward, starched uniform, not a wrinkle to be seen. She could've sworn it was Trent who pulled up behind her—or had she imagined it? Assumed?

Holly stepped out under the judging eye of this cop she'd never seen. "I'm sorry. I don't think we've ever met."

The cop said nothing, her face expressionless, eyes cold.

Holly giggled, more out of nerves, knowing this wasn't the right response. "I know. You want one of my cheesecakes? There in the back."

Not even a hint of smile. "Are you bribing an officer of the law?"

"No, Ma'am. I mean, Sir. I mean, Ma'am." She briefly closed her eyes, hoping, wishing, she were anywhere, even Alaska during a blizzard. "Are you new on the force? I'm new to town and thought I'd met most of the police."

"I'm Chief Hardy." She offered Holly a curt nod. "Walk a straight line, please."

What? She had to be kidding. At the most, Holly had a glass of wine per week. The sinking sun told her it was afternoon. "I am not a lush, thank you very much.

"Walk a straight line. Toe to toe, please."

"Could you call Officer Trinket?"

"Ma'am. I suggest you follow orders."

Stifling the huff, Holly put her arms out and walked toe to toe. She wobbled once, more due to nerves than anything.

"Place your arms out and then touch your fingers to your nose, respectively."

Holly obeyed. "Seriously. Officer Trinket can vouch for me."

"Why were you visiting the Poppletons?"

"I'm sorry. I think we got off on the wrong foot. I never should've tried to outrun you but I thought you were Trent and you see..." Holly couldn't finish her thought because she hadn't really thought that far. If she'd thought it wasn't

Trent, she would've pulled over right away. She forced a smile. "I'm new in town. Owner of *Just Cheesecake*. You should stop by for a slice. On the house."

Chief Hardy raised an eyebrow.

"I mean stop by but not in a bribe sort of way. In fact, forget on the house. You're more than welcome to pay full price or more if you'd like. Or don't stop by at all. It doesn't matter—"

"Answer the question, please."

"Um, what was the question again?" Holly asked, more humiliated than she'd ever been, even when she messed up her oral report in seventh grade.

"There's a murder investigation right now. You were named as a potential suspect. Yet you visit the Poppletons. Why?"

How could Holly explain that she was trying to clear her name? That she was involved in a secret detective society that supported the local police department. That Officer Trinket knew and trusted her. "Maybe if you call Officer Trinket?"

"I'd like to hear it from you, Ms. Hart. I don't care what Officer Trinket has to say about it."

"I was offering my condolences on the loss of their grandmother."

"Why? Did you know them personally?"

"Well, no, not really. I met them the other night. Nice family." Holly tittered. "Well, not as nice as I first thought."

"Are you assuming the murder was the outcome of a personal nature, a family feud?"

Holly had a feeling that the cop was playing games, trying to trap her into saying something wrong.

"Or are you desperate?" Chief Hardy stepped closer. "You killed the old lady and before you land in jail are trying to frame them? Leave evidence behind in their house?"

"Absolutely not!" Holly almost shouted. "Excuse me. But I don't think it's your job to accuse innocent people of murder. You are crossing the line here."

"Fine." She smirked. "Let's take this downtown." She pushed Holly against the car and cuffed her. With a firm grip, she led Holly to the back of the cruiser.

On the drive to town, Holly fumed. Okay, she'd admit it! Nerves got the better of her. She spoke out of line. She never should've mentioned Trent's name but politely answer the questions instead. Apologized.

They pulled up just as the door to the police station swung open and Millicent strode out, camera swinging by her side. Holly ground her teeth, knowing exactly what would happen.

Chief Hardy led her into the station. Millicent smirked and took her picture. Terrific. Another wonderful article coming right up like an order of eggs sunnyside up. When she entered the station, reality hit. Hardy could keep her here for hours. What if she was charged with bribing an officer? Could she do that?

***

MILLICENT'S HEELS TAPPED on the pavement. The quick, sharp sound echoed inside Holly's head. Why couldn't she just leave well enough alone? Go bother someone else?

"Excuse me!" Millicent called, her voice high and friendly.

Chief Hardy ignored her. She pushed on the door and nudged Holly into the station. The stale smell of coffee held bad memories. She was always here under suspicious motivations. She made a promise, that when this investigation was all over, she'd return, spend the day here and forge positive associations with the smell of bitter, burnt coffee.

"Take a seat," Hardy ordered. "Might as well get comfortable. This could take a while."

Holly clamped her mouth shut and perched on the edge of a plastic chair. Hardy was playing unfair, keeping her on purpose, as punishment. Of course, Trent was most likely out at the Poppletons, investigating.

The new chief stood behind the desk, ruffling papers, probably looking for the keys to lock her up.

"Excuse me." Millicent approached the desk. "I wanted to introduce myself. I'm Millicent Monroe, star reporter for the Fairview Paper."

Holly snorted. She didn't mean to. She'd been clenching her mouth shut so she wouldn't give either of them ammunition.

Chief Hardy didn't miss a beat. Her eyes narrowed, gleamed with amusement. "Nice to meet you, Ms. Monroe. What can I do for you?"

Millicent beamed. She leaned in and whispered, "I couldn't help but notice that you brought in Holly Hart." Millicent gave her a sideways glance. "This isn't the first time she's been questioned or suspected in a murder investigation."

"Is that so? Thank you for passing that information along. Is there anything else?"

"My duty is to the people of this town. I'm off to type up my article now. Is there anything the townspeople need to know? Any new news?"

Hardy crossed her arms and studied Holly, who stared right back at her. "Why yes, I do think the town could benefit from what happened today. We'll just say that a citizen of Fairview thought it would be fun to have a little car chase and then bribe the officer on duty."

Millicent gasped. "No!"

"Let the people know that even though their new chief is a woman, they're going to wish I was a man when I start cracking down on crime, from parking tickets to murder."

"Can I quote you on that?" Millicent's pencil flew across her notepad.

Chief Hardy nodded her approval. "Now if you don't mind, I have a mound of paperwork to complete, and I'd like to be home before midnight."

Midnight? Holly deflated, slumping back in her chair. How did this day go so horribly wrong? She desperately craved hot tea and something sweet. Muffins! How could she forget about him? "Am I allowed a phone call?"

"You're not under arrest, Ms. Hart."

"Then why the cuffs?"

"I'll let you figure that one out."

Holly kept her eyes on Millicent as she flounced toward the door, bursting with excitement over the chief's statement and her future article on Holly. Right as she had her hand on the door, about to leave, Holly called, "Millicent?"

Millicent hesitated, then slowly turned, the surprise written on her face that Holly talked to her. "Don't even think about bribing me with cheesecake instead of doing my duty to the town of Fairview. First of all, I have access to all the cheesecake I want. Better than the fluff and stuff you try to pass off as cheesecake."

"I need a favor." Holly said it quietly, her words barely penetrating Millicent's chatter.

"Ha! Forget it. I'm not going to let your little boy toy know you're here. You can't just sweep into town and steal everything I've worked for over the years."

What? Steal everything? She thought about Millicent's sugary conversation with Trent, the way she traced his cheek. Had they dated? She'd have to ask Charlene if and when she ever got out of here. They'd all be at her apartment tonight for book club. They might be waiting for a long time.

Millicent stood, her foot tapping as she looked down at Holly.

"I left Muffins in my car over near Hilltop Drive. Could you please make sure he's okay? Drop him off at my apartment? You'll find my keys back in my car. I'd appreciate it."

"Humph. You're just lucky I love animals." Then she flounced out of the station.

The next few hours passed slowly, time creeping by. Holly dozed several times but the cuffs chafed her wrists and grew uncomfortable. Chief Hardy sat behind the desk, working. Finally, much later, darkness swallowing any natural light outside, the chief approached her. "Did you figure it out?" she asked.

"You mean about the cuffs?" Holly shifted uncomfortably and stifled a yawn.

"Yes. What did you learn today?"

"Not to mess with Chief Hardy."

The hint of a smile flickered. "I like that." She unlocked the cuffs. "Just because I'm a woman doesn't mean I'm a pushover. The sooner everyone learns that the better."

Holly rubbed her wrists. "Yes, Ma'am."

Time for book club. Time for the secret society to pool together the information learned today and solve a murder.

And did she ever have a lot to share. About the Poppletons and their neighbors and the new Chief Hardy.

HOLLY COULD BARELY keep her eyes open when she trudged up the steps to her apartment. Maybe she should cancel book club. Her bed called. Her soft covers, silky sheets. A few chapters of a mystery novel and she'd be out. She fumbled with the key only to find the door unlocked.

Hesitantly, she opened the door.

"Look who finally arrived to her own party." Charlene sat at the table. "Book club started a couple hours ago. Remember what I said about commitment. When you are part of this club, it's a priority."

At every reprimand and reminder, Holly nodded.

"Oh, shush," Kitty interrupted. "Can't you see something happened to this girl?" She cleared her throat. "Ladies, she needs the treatment."

"Oh, fine," Charlene muttered. "But I'm not rubbing her feet."

"Wait!" Holly searched the room. "Where's Muffins?"

"Curled up on his doggy bed," Charlene said. "And by the way, your room's a mess."

"Okay. At least he's back." Millicent had followed through on the favor.

They moved into action. Kitty poured a glass of red wine and handed it to Holly, then led her over to the couch. Ann massaged her shoulders. Charlene pulled a classic Agatha Christie novel from her bag and flipped to the last chapter. As she read, the words of mystery and intrigue calmed Holly. She relaxed. Almost fell asleep.

"Okay, then. We ready to get down to business?" Charlene asked.

"Wow. Thank you. Such hospitality in my own house too."

Kitty smiled and patted her leg. "It's a long story. It started when Ann was held hostage for an afternoon. She was the first to receive the treatment."

Ann nodded, grinning.

"What happened to you?" Charlene pointed a finger at Holly,

Had it just been that morning that they'd held an emergency meeting at *Just Cheesecake*? It felt like a week ago. "I met Chief Hardy."

"Ouch. I meant to warn you about her." Charlene screwed up her face. "It didn't go well?"

"I thought she was Trent, so I didn't pull over right away, and then I gave her sass. She put me through the entire sobriety test and dragged me down to the station in cuffs."

The room fell silent. It started with a snort and then a giggle. Soon they were laughing. Holly pulled back her hair in a perfect imitation of Chief Hardy. "No one messes with Chief Hardy."

Their laughter subsided, and in the quiet, Ann asked, "Why did she pull you over?"

"I was leaving the Poppletons. She was arriving. Something about messing with an investigation."

"The Poppletons?" Charlene exploded. "Why didn't you tell us? Spill it. Tell us everything."

Holly explained about her meeting with Andrea Givingsworth, the neighbor. That Andrea mentioned her neighbor and murder and something about a large inheritance. Then, Holly talked about the Poppletons. Clara, Donovan, and Derek. And that yes, Derek let slip about their big inheritance. "So there definitely seems to be motive. Enough that I shouldn't even be on the suspect list."

"Good work," Charlene said. Ann and Kitty nodded in agreement. "Ann, what did you learn at the library?"

They jumped at a loud banging on the door. Holly braced herself. What if Chief Hardy had followed her home? That woman would be in her nightmares for weeks.

"I know you're in there," Millicent called. "I know it's a mystery club."

"You've been removed from the club, if you don't remember," Charlene yelled.

Holly placed her head in her hands and groaned.

"I'm calling in a favor! Just ask Holly about it."

Charlene, Kitty, and Ann all looked at her.

Holly shrugged. "I had no one else to help. Chief Hardy wouldn't let me call anyone. Millicent was there so I asked her to drive out to my car and get Muffins."

"I rescued her dog and so I want back in the club!"

Charlene tromped over and opened the door. "Why?"

"Why what?" Millicent asked. Her blonde pixie cut was rather disheveled, her eyes wide and innocent.

"Why do you want back in the club?"

"I love mysteries. Just like all of you." She sniffed. "I miss talking about them."

"Fine. A favor is a favor."

Minutes later they were gathered in Holly's living room. Millicent observed, her gaze taking everything in, the lack of appetizers.

"Where's the food?" she asked. "I stop coming and the whole club falls apart."

"Too involved in discussing mysteries, I guess." Holly shrugged and glanced at Charlene. They'd been too involved in this latest murder to even read, never mind talk about motive and guilt of fictional characters.

Charlene pulled out the Agatha Christie as if they'd been discussing it the whole evening.

"That one again?" Millicent asked. "We reread that one last year."

"Oh, it's my favorite," Holly gushed.

"We wanted to read it again," Ann piped in.

They talked about red herrings, hard clues, soft clues, hidden clues, motive, intent. Millicent joined in at first, but then fell silent, observing, listening.

Charlene discussed at length the symbolism and theme. Kitty went on about the character development of the murderer. Ann nodded enthusiastically to everything. Holly should be tired enough to snooze through the whole thing, but she wanted to know what Ann discovered at the library. The big news story with the Poppletons years ago could be the key to cracking this case wide open.

Two hours later, Charlene cracked her knuckles and then attempted to brush cat hair off her shirt. "I guess maybe we should call it a night."

"Oh my," Millicent said, her innocent comment a little too innocent. "Time flew by."

Ann chewed her nail, glanced at the clock, then at Millicent, then back at all of them. They were cleaning up the wineglasses when she blurted. "I think...the detective...in this novel...should've done more research at the library." She put careful emphasis on her last word. "She might've realized that news in the past would confirm everything about the current suspicions."

Holly placed her glass in the sink, her back turned. She knew it! At some point in the past, the Poppletons had a big enough family brouhaha that it made the news. She'd learn the details later. The large family had motive.

"I knew it!" Millicent banged her fist on the table. "This wasn't a book club at all. You guys were so obvious."

Charlene moved to the door. "Not this nonsense about a secret club again. Really Millicent. If you spent as much time pounding the keys for that mystery novel of yours as you do going on about your conspiracy theories, you'd be a published author by now."

Hurt flickered on her face, but she quickly masked it. "You can play this however you want, but I'm not stupid." She directed her next comment to Holly. "And next time? Forget it. Your stupid little dog can die for all I care." Then she left, slamming the door.

"Nice one," Charlene grumbled.

"I'm sorry. Everyone was going to leave. It took hours but I found the article. It wasn't long. Easy to overlook. One of Agatha's sons tried to take over the family estate, claiming his mother mentally incompetent. His efforts failed."

"Ah, but now we have strong motive," Charlene stated.

PALE PINK STREAMS of color lit up the early morning air. The sun still hid behind the line of trees. The coolness of a summer morning brought a smile to Holly's face as she crossed the street to *Just Cheesecake*.

"Today is going to be an easy day," she told herself. "I'll bake and prepare for the Givingsworth party tomorrow. That's it."

She grabbed her key ring and immediately noticed the missing key. The key to *Just Cheesecake*. Ignoring the paranoid suspicion that someone stole it, she jogged back to her apartment and grabbed the spare key, promising to search for the missing one later.

The parking lot was empty, the town practically deserted. Too early even for the early birds. Except for Charlene standing by her door.

"About time you got here. I've been waiting for hours."

Holly tapped her watch. "Hours?"

"Details, details. Fine. I arrived a few minutes ago. I had a feeling you'd be here at an indecent hour. And I figured you wouldn't tell me either. And I was right."

"Just because I put in extra hours doesn't mean you have to." Holly unlocked the door.

"You think I came just to help you bake cheesecakes?" Charlene followed, clomping across the tiles floor in her yellow boots. "We need to talk strategy. And you need to tell me everything else that happened yesterday."

Holly wasn't surprised that Charlene surmised there was more. The meeting of the mystery minds the night before had been cut short by the blonde bimbo. Then, it had been too late. The day had been too exhausting.

"What do you want to know?" Holly handed Charlene an apron, then slid hers over her head. A flick of the switch and light flooded the kitchen. She pulled her pre-made mixes from the freezer. This would definitely speed the process along.

"What happened to our plan yesterday. You were supposed to cause a scene at *The Tasty Bite*. Trent was supposed to break it up."

Holly raised an eyebrow at her friend. "I suppose you thought it would be happily ever after for Trent and me while you snooped in his office?"

"Something like that." Charlene pulled out the springform pans and muffin tins. "We doing the usual?"

"Yup." Holly wanted her minis and her full eight-inch cakes for the party. A taste of everything.

They worked in silence, mixing the different batters, filling the pans, and sliding them into the large oven. With the various fruit sauces bubbling on the stovetop, Holly stretched. "How about some coffee?"

"Sure thing. Then you'll talk?" Charlene headed to the Keurig.

"Yes, I'll tell you everything." As soon as they were seated at one of the tables, mugs in hand, Holly said, "Let's start with Pierre."

"What about the old geezer?"

"He's too nice. I couldn't yell at one of the kindest, nicest men in town." Holly thought back on Millicent's conversation with Trent. "And then there was the tiny fact that Millicent had your son wrapped so tightly around her little finger that I wasn't sure he'd do anything but sit under her spell." Holly sipped the hazelnut coffee. She made the decision to keep Trent's secret to herself. That he knew about their secret society. That he played along with Charlene's games, letting her believe she had him fooled.

"Millicent?" Charlene asked, the annoyance showing in her tone. "That girl's been after him since high school."

"High school?"

"That's right. She hasn't stopped hoping ever since he broke up with her after graduation. She'd played too many games, told too many lies. But let's not get off track. Anything else I need to know?"

"After talking with the Poppletons and their neighbors, I found one thing rather odd. They cast suspicion on each other."

Charlene lit with excitement. "Which means we'll have to search both their houses for traces of poison."

"Haven't the cops already done that?" Holly asked.

"Yes, but we have newer information. Past trouble with the Poppletons concerning inheritance money. Nosy neighbors quick to accuse. We can look for poison, but we'll be searching for other clues too. We'll know when we see it."

Holly made plans to meet Charlene early afternoon, after she ate lunch and walked Muffins. Then that would be it for sleuthing. She needed a long afternoon of watching mystery reruns.

She pulled her cakes from the oven, let them cool, and added the sauces. Perfection. After sliding them into the fridge for the next day, she headed over to *Oodles*.

"Hi, Lindsey!" Holly walked up to the counter.

"Hey, there. You look beat." Lindsey pulled out a new stack of to-go coffee cups.

"I am. It's been a long couple days. Think I might need one of your BLTs."

"Sure thing. You go on and take a seat, and someone will be over in a second."

"Thanks." She turned to find a seat in the sun by a window and almost ran into Millicent.

"The daily paper's fresh from print. It's my best yet."

"That's good." Holly walked right past to a table. She wasn't up for Millicent or articles that spewed lies.

Millicent followed, sticking to her like flies to fly paper. She even had the gall to take the seat across from Holly.

"What do you want?" Holly sighed.

"Your turn will fade, you know."

"What's that supposed to mean?" She was tired of games.

"Meaning I used to be the golden girl. I was the young star of the murder mystery book club." She held out her fingers spaced an inch apart. "I was this close to being asked into their stupid mystery society. Until you moved to town."

The waitress arrived, and Holly placed her order. "I have no idea what you're talking about."

"Yes, you do. And I would've been perfect. I'm an investigative reporter. Much more experienced than you when it comes to hunting down clues." She leaned forward, the words hissing out of her mouth. "It should've been me." Then with a look of disdain, Millicent walked away.

Holly ate her sandwich, except it was hard to enjoy. Everything she'd learned today spoke to the truth of what Millicent said. That Holly had taken her place. Combined with the fact that *Just Cheesecake* competed with Millicent's father's business—Holly understood her dislike.

The midday sun beat through the window. The warmth relaxed Holly, and she sat, sipping her water, zoning out. Enjoying a moment of thinking about nothing. It didn't last long.

Donovan Poppleton stepped out of his car.

Forget the nap. Time to do a little espionage.

***

HOLLY PAID HER bill, left a generous tip, then walked outside. Heat shimmered off the road, the humidity levels high. Mom and Pop shops lined both sides of Main Street. They drew plenty of customers from tourists and townspeople. Moms with strollers. Men and women on lunch break, out for some fresh air. Teenagers on skateboards or walking in groups.

But Donovan seemed to have disappeared.

She should go home and search for her shop key but a tingle of anticipation ran up her spine, confirming she was onto something. She took to the sidewalk, losing herself in the crowds while keeping a casual eye out for Donovan. Finally, when she was about to give up and go back for

Muffins, Donovan ducked into an old house that had been converted into office buildings.

Closer, her heart beat faster when she noticed the sign. Stern & Stern Law Offices. Interesting. When the front door opened and a client walked out, she slid inside. Perfect timing. No one sat behind the front desk, the place seemingly empty except for Donovan's voice reverberating from an office nearby. The entire place was formal in a lawyerish kind of way with a striped loveseat and matching armchair in the waiting area. She sat on the loveseat and strained to catch what they were saying. Why couldn't people have important meetings with doors open? They had to be talking about the family will and money.

At the click clack of heels, the secretary returning from a break or the bathroom, Holly slumped, hoping to remain unseen. It worked at first until someone spotted her.

"Holly? Is that you?"

Donovan.

She shot up. "Oh, hi. Yes, it's me. Holly." She laughed. It faded quickly, and they were left with awkward silence. That of course, had to be filled. "I'm here to see about a living will. Everything this week has started me thinking."

He smiled. "Oh, right. Don't blame you. It's never too early to start. Just a word of advice. No need to keep your will a secret. Let your family know about it."

Holly glanced between the secretary, who frowned over her glasses, and Donovan. She didn't want to lose her chance. "Maybe you'd be willing to offer some advice? It all seems a bit overwhelming." Sometimes youth had an advantage.

"Sure. Why don't we grab some ice cream and talk? I was hoping to find you anyway. Something I wanted to talk to you about."

Holly had told herself no sleuthing today. This afternoon was supposed to be about napping and movies. But how could she say no?

"SOUNDS GREAT." SHE walked toward the door with him. "Today's a boiler, for sure."

The ice cream shop was just down the street, a few shops away. The Arctic Express had a window to order soft serve or hard ice cream.

"Wow. I thought for sure the line would be out the door," Holly said.

"Maybe we got lucky and hit a lull."

Holly ordered salted caramel, and Donovan ordered strawberry. Minutes later, they sat on a bench that looked over the town green.

"Strawberry?" Holly asked. "Isn't that kind of boring? They had a zillion flavors."

"I suppose so. Sometimes simple and classic is best."

"True." Holly searched her mind for conversation starters that wouldn't sound like she was a reporter or a complete amateur. Donovan was a stranger. Some people are hyper sensitive to questions. "Simple and classic, huh?" Yup. Way to go, Holly thought.

Donovan licked at a stream of ice cream already running down the side of the cone. "Simple and classic and straightforward. That's how I would describe myself. My family would agree. My wife and kids. From the way I approach relationships to cars to decorating. Nothing too fancy."

Yet, Holly thought. His family came from money. Sometimes simple and classic didn't mean cheap. Maybe his lifestyle needed funding?

"That's why I think wills and matters of inheritance shouldn't be kept in secret. Surprising families after the person has passed away."

Holly spoke softly. "I'm guessing your family was surprised?"

"You could say that." The stream ran from the cone onto his arm. "Geez. I feel like a six year old."

Holly licked her cone. "I know what you mean. It's this heat!" Darn that melting ice cream. She wanted to hear more about how Agatha Poppleton surprised her family.

"When you go back to make your living will. I suggest you keep it simple, for now, and let your loved ones know exactly what's in it."

"Aren't there good reasons though for keeping those matters secret? Like not causing bad feelings between family members while you're alive?"

His expression darkened. "That could happen. But then the person would be around to offer explanations."

Holly had a feeling this conversation was no longer hypothetical. She prodded gently. "I'm sorry your family is going through such a hard time. I guess this stuff is never easy."

"That's for sure." He popped the last bite into his mouth. "My brother, Derek, is never easy to deal with, never has been. Our neighbors are definitely not making this any easier."

"What do you mean?" Holly leaned back, trying to act like whether he answered or not wasn't important.

"They're blaming us for destroying their rock garden, wall, whatever it is. When anything could have knocked it down. The weather. A black bear." He leaned his elbows on his knees, taking in the town, not saying anything.

"Why would they blame you?" Holly leaned forward too. She remembered the perfection of the Givingsworth's house and lawn. The stone wall matched the rest, except for the one section. It hadn't looked like a rainstorm or wild animal could cause that much damage. But what did she know?

"I have no idea," he said, then clamped shut, almost as if he did have an idea but wasn't sharing it. Seconds later, he forced a laugh. "But you don't want to hear all about my family affair. We've caused you enough trouble. Are the police still giving you a hard time?"

Holly shuddered just thinking about Chief Hardy.

"That bad?"

"No, not really. They've pretty much ruled me out. I hope."

His cheeks turned pink. "About that. Derek can be a jerk. I wanted to apologize to you for him. The way he talked

127

to you earlier at our house when you were just dropping by to offer your condolences. It was awful. His wife Clara isn't much better."

"No problem. I understand." Their family was ripe with tension. Derek pointed the finger at everyone. At her. At his neighbors. When someone's redirecting...maybe it's because they don't want the spotlight on them. A destroyed rock wall is not strong enough motivation for murder. Unless there was more to the story. More to the neighborly conflict. Or more backstory to the Poppleton family conflict.

"So we're forgiven?" he asked.

"Definitely." Forgiven but not forgotten, Holly added silently. She wanted to ask more about Derek, more about the will and the big surprise. Maybe if she asked for more tips on wills the conversation would go back his family."

Before Holly could broach it, Donovan stood. "Hope I was able to help." He glanced at his watch. "Time for family drama."

"Oh?"

"A memorial luncheon, and then a family meeting with a lawyer to figure out what needs to be done." He crumpled his napkin. "Have a nice afternoon."

"You too." Holly stayed on the bench, her hands and mouth sticky with melted ice cream. Sweat dripped down her back, between her shoulder blades, but not just from the heat. The whole conversation with Donovan, her adrenaline ran high, her blood thrumming through her veins. Any second, she expected him to see through her questions. Thankfully, he didn't.

He left her with so much to process.

Like the fact that he would be at a family luncheon and then a family meeting with the lawyer. Combined, those two events could take hours. Leaving enough time for her to slip in and out and search for clues.

Nope. No way. Never.

She stood and strode toward home. This afternoon was set aside for non-sleuthing activities. She needed it. The thought pushed from her mind, she ran through her list of movies and books. Holly forced herself to think about that.

By the time she reached home, she needed a shower. Muffins needed a walk. Instead, a note was on her door.

Meet me at the station.

Trent.

Holly crumpled the note. Maybe this was Trent's way of being romantic. Maybe this had nothing to do with the murder investigation. Maybe this had nothing to do with Chief Hardy.

A shudder rippled through her.

Well, too bad. The new chief would give her nightmares for weeks. And meeting at a police station was not romantic!

She unlocked and went inside. After refreshing Muffins' water bowl and giving him some loving, she took a shower. She folded laundry. She vacuumed.

Enough was enough. She texted Charlene. *Important. Meet me at my house.*

***

CHARLENE PLOPPED A huge duffel bag on Holly's kitchen table. It made a loud clunk.

"What do you have in there? Your entire garage?" Holly asked.

"This is my bag of magic tricks. Everything needed for an afternoon of sleuthing, collected over the years by yours truly. Fake mustaches, wigs, costumes, pepper spray. You name it."

Holly caught Charlene up to date on their short window of opportunity in the next few hours. Then, she tapped the duffel bag. "I'm not going undercover. I'm breaking in. Looking like Sherlock Holmes is not going to help me find any clues or poison any better or faster than if dressed as myself."

"Humph. You might have a point." She rifled through her bag and pulled out a small lace satchel. "Then you'll need this."

Suspicious, Holly pulled at the strings, allowing the satchel to fall open. She pulled out a small track phone, an audio recorder, tiny flashlight, a knife, chewing gum, pepper spray, a granola bar and a water bottle."

Most of it Holly could understand. "A track phone?"

"In case ours are bugged. I wouldn't put anything past my son or the new chief."

"Granola bar?"

Charlene shrugged. "You never know. You've got to be prepared for anything." She zipped the bag. "Aren't you going to ask about the lace satchel?"

Holly laughed. "That's obvious. I can pretend it's my purse."

"I knew there was a reason we invited you into the society. Now, when did you talk to Donovan?"

"About an hour ago."

Charlene paled. "You're wasting time, then. Get going."
She almost sprinted to the front door. I'll drop you off and
circle the neighborhood. In thirty minutes, I'll be back. You
know my philosophy."

"Get out sooner than later."

THE DUST CHARLENE'S truck kicked up as she drove away choked Holly's throat.

The Poppleton house towered over her, bigger than she remembered. More ominous. Charlene gave specific instructions. This was rural New Hampshire. Front door would be locked, but side windows wouldn't be. Lift one up, remove the screen, and climb inside. And pray that they lived far enough out that they didn't worry about security systems.

Once inside, look for poison.

Hunt for anything suspicious. Letters. Photos.

Check the office for a copy of the will.

Check the home computer but don't spend time guessing at a passcode if one's set up.

Get in. Get out.

With a glance around, already feeling guilty, she strolled across the lawn as if she belonged here. Just in case a delivery truck rolled in or a neighbor stopped by. Once she reached the house, she crept along the front and rounded to the side facing the woods. There weren't many trees between this house and the Givingsworth's. If she peered carefully, she could make out a bit of color. In the winter it would be transparent.

Charlene was right. The window wasn't locked, except it was slightly higher off the ground than she expected. No possibly way she could leap and make it. Feeling the pressure and slightly panicked at the passing time, Holly dashed to the backyard and the flower garden. Among the flowering bushes and rock garden sat a gnome with a twisted white beard, red hat, and big belly.

"You'll have to do. Sorry old chum."

She grabbed him and raced back to the window. Screwing the point of his hat into the mulch, Holly made sure he was steady by pushing mulch around his body for support. She stepped onto the bottom of his feet and reached up to push up the window.

Just as she went to pull out the screen the gnome wobbled. With a small gasp, she crashed forward, warping the screen, her body scraping against the windowsill.

She could leave now but the damage had been done. One foot in front of the other, Holly climbed through and landed on soft carpet. The room smelled of old books, dust, and air freshener. An office. There was just enough light to see. First on the list was the computer, which sat nice and shiny on a desk in the corner. She tapped at the keyboard and the screen brightened.

A username password popped up, so she moved onto the drawers. Nice, smooth wood drawers that opened easily. Agatha ran a clean, organized office. In the first drawer was a copy of the will. Holly laid it on the desk, her eyes skimming the legalese for a clue. She found it on the fourth page.

Beneficiaries: Donovan Poppleton. Derek Poppleton. Darla Poppleton.

Click. She took a picture.

All the children. Two brothers and a sister Holly hadn't met yet. She thought back to her conversation with

Donovan. He suggested a will that was easy and straightforward. He suggested she talk to her loved ones so there were no surprises. Was it a surprise that their mother evenly divided her estate? Shouldn't be. That would be expected.

She flipped back and read the earlier pages. From the looks of it, there was no massive fortune. Mainly the house. But wasn't that worth a lot? Was it worth fighting over? Was it enough motivation for murder?

What was the shocking surprise?

With a sigh, she re-filed the will and placed it back in the drawer. Time to investigate the rest of the house. Get in. Get out. She had about twenty minutes left.

Where would someone store poison?

She headed to the pantry, then the furnace room, then the bedrooms. She looked in underwear drawers and through big granny panties. Nothing. She searched the guest bedrooms and closets and under the beds.

Nothing suspicious. Unless a hidden bottle of whiskey counted. Holly unscrewed the top and sniffed. Definitely whiskey.

Light on her feet and moving fast, she went room to room downstairs. Wasn't a clue supposed to pop out at her?

That was how it worked in books and movies. She spotted a pile of mail on the kitchen counter. Of course, not all important letters were kept in the office. She made it through the top four until she came to envelope with just a name on it scribbled with pen.

Agatha.

That was it. Except it was unopened. Had no one noticed it yet?

She slid her finger across and lifted the flap. With so many people living here, any one could've opened it. Even Agatha, who was no longer around to say differently. With a glance over her shoulder, Holly shrugged off the guilt and the creepy factor. Maybe that was a sign to get out.

She skimmed the letter. The writing was loopy and cursive, suggesting an older generation. Like a certain neighbor.

This has gone on long enough, Agatha. It's time for you to return what is rightfully ours. Richard is no longer here. I know you've always wanted to do the right thing.

Thank you,
Andrea

A car door slammed.

She raced back toward the office but the front door opened, so she halted and slid on the floor. She couldn't dash into the office without someone walking through the front door seeing her. At the last second, she dove into a hall closet and shut the door. She scooted toward the back and pulled the ends of long coats in front of her.

How had she lost track of time?

People argued. Their voices, strained and tired, were filled with tension. She recognized Donovan, Derek, and Clara. The screams and banging and running of their children made it impossible to understand anything more than a few words.

How long would they be here? Would she have to wait until night to leave?

"Derek!" Clara screeched. "Call the cops."

Holly curled into a ball and leaned her forehead against her knees. They must've found the open window and broken screen. Somehow Charlene's easy plan went wrong fast.

Sweaty, scared, and feeling slightly claustrophobic, Holly sat in the darkness. The cops would be coming. Soon. They'd probably search the closet. What if it was Chief

Hardy? What if it was Trent? Both would most likely throw her in a cell for the night. To teach her a lesson.

She had to find the right time to sneak out.

The cops arrived, car doors shut. Raised voices demanded justice.

"The murderer was back."

"Can't you do something? We need round-the-clock protection."

Holly huffed at that. A warped screen didn't mean murder. It could've been a local teen screwing around with friends in the heat of summer.

Footsteps passed, and Holly held her breath. They headed toward the office and the evidence.

Now! While they were occupied.

Shaking, Holly stood, gently turned the knob, and moved the door slowly. She peeked out. Nothing. The coast was clear. This was the worst idea she'd ever had.

Praying for a shot of good luck, she stepped into the hallway. A clear path led to the sliding glass door that opened into the backyard. The sharp and stern Chief Hardy asked Donovan and Derek questions. Holly tiptoed to the door.

She unlocked it and slid it open. A wave of heat hit her face, but it smelled like freedom. She didn't even bother closing the door but took off around the other side of the house. She flew across the grass, gaining speed. Charlene should be around her somewhere. Holly was half-sobbing half-laughing like a maniac when she turned the corner and ran into someone.

Trent.

At first, they stared at each other. Shocked.

His eyes narrowed. "What are you doing here?" Then understanding dawned. Holly saw it in his eyes. At first anger sparked then faded to sadness. "This was you and my mother. Wasn't it?"

"No. Just me." The lies stumbled out easily. Too easily. "I ran into Donovan earlier and something he said made me suspicious. I figured you'd tell me to stop snooping and I hated to see a possible clue get lost in the investigation and, and..."

"Just go. Now." Then he brushed past her into the house.

∗∗∗

BACK AT HOME, snuggling under a blanket—more for comfort than heat, Holly nibbled on the emergency granola

140

bar. She clutched her phone, hoping Trent would text or call, hoping to God he wouldn't. Every time she thought of him all she could see was the betrayal etched onto his face, the way he spoke, the way he brushed past her.

Charlene had picked up Holly half a mile from the Poppleton house. In as few words as possible, Holly told her partner in crime that the will showed nothing. All the children were beneficiaries. Nothing that made them appear guilty.

She'd told Charlene about the letter from Andrea and that the neighbor wanted something she believed was hers, but she didn't say a word about Trent. That she'd majorly goofed and their whole investigation was compromised, their society possibly over. Trent would see to that. The rest of the car ride was silent. Charlene seemed to know Holly needed alone time.

At Holly's apartment, she'd patted Holly's leg. "You did good. Rest up. Tomorrow will be another big day."

Tomorrow. A chance to nose around at the Givingsworth house, and possibly find a motive for murder. Find out what Andrea thought the Poppleton's owed her.

Her granola bar gone, and in need of more comfort food, Holly noticed it. The key. Her key to *Just Cheesecake*. The one missing on her key ring.

It sat, shiny and silver, on the kitchen table. Like it had been misplaced instead of lost. Like it had been a careless mistake, instead of a purposeful action.

Holly ran her finger over the smooth metal. With grim determination and a sinking feeling, she headed over to *Just Cheesecake*. Not sure of what she'd find but knowing she had to look.

16

WITH A DEEP BREATH, Holly turned her back on *Just Cheesecake*. A feeling of dread lingered and wouldn't go away, ever since she found the missing key to her shop, lying on the kitchen table. She'd never taken the key off her key ring. Keys don't magically appear or disappear unless someone messes with them. She had an idea who, but couldn't, wouldn't let her mind go there.

Fairview in the summer wore evening well. The heat of day turned to pleasant warmth. Soft colors of sunset made the atmosphere romantic. The sidewalks were filled with joggers, walkers, and casual strollers. *Oodles* and *Gotcha*, the gift store on the other side of *Just Cheesecake*, were bustling with business. She doubted her business plan. Maybe she should be open more than three days a week? Then she thought of all the hours that would keep her from filling large custom orders—that's where the money lay. That's the customer base she needed. Her cheesecake company wasn't trying to compete with *The Tasty Bite*. So why was Millicent turning it into a battle?

Time to check out *Just Cheesecake*. No more stalling.

Her first step inside resulted in a small breath of relief. All the baked goods were still in the glass showcase. Everything was in order—the tables, chairs, and coffee table.

She walked through into the kitchen. Cinnamon and sugar still scented the air. The still and quiet almost creeped her out. But everything remained in order. Had the stolen key been a product of her imagination? Maybe Charlene had borrowed it to tidy up or clean the floor.

Maybe.

The feeling remained, and Holly wouldn't be able to sleep peacefully until checking the fridge and freezer. She opened the fridge first, to check on her beauties for the

Givingsworth party tomorrow. Cold air nipped her cheeks as she gazed upon the mini and full-sized cheesecakes.

Her skin tingled, and heat raced through her as she battled between rage and utter devastation. Each cake had been mashed, ruined, only good to throw out. In a matter of minutes, someone had destroyed hours of work.

She fumbled for her phone and punched in Charlene's number, briefly explaining what had happened. Ten minutes later, someone knocked on the front door. Slowly, she trudged to let Charlene inside.

"I brought reinforcements," Charlene said.

Kitty and Ann walked in behind her. Kitty carried a bottle of wine, and Ann held a container of homemade cookies. As Holly told them her theory and the state of her work and the possible loss in revenue, Kitty poured the wine.

"What a shame," Ann whispered.

"Someone destroys and tears down when they're jealous and feel threatened," Kitty stated as if that provided all the answers.

Holly blinked back the tears, refusing to give in to them. "I haven't threatened anyone!"

Charlene raised an eyebrow, questioning her without having to say the words.

Holly thought about *The Tasty Bite*, Millicent's articles, the Fourth of July fiasco. And most of all…Trent. "Fine. But not on purpose."

"There's only one thing to do." Charlene drained her wineglass.

"What?" they asked together.

"We multi-task." A grim look, in the set of Charlene's jaw, the determination in her eyes, conveyed her intentions. "While we recount the facts of the murder, see if we missed anything, we'll get an assembly line going like we did before the Fourth, and replace all the desserts needed for the event tomorrow."

Holly wanted to refuse. It was late. Charlene's suggestion would take hours, but then she saw their smiles, their willingness to help, and she couldn't turn them down. "Thank you," she whispered.

They got to work. Holly and Charlene mixed up the cheesecake filling, while Ann started the glazes. Kitty crushed Oreos, set out the pans, and kept the wineglasses filled.

They went back to the night of the Fourth, recounting the important details. The Poppletons were there, the whole family. Possibly in for the holiday weekend. Agatha sat watching. The last time Holly spoke with her was to sell her family the fresh fruit tortes. At that time, she was alive, conversing with her family.

"Now I know it was Derek who engaged Agatha in what appeared to be repetitive, tiresome conversation. Clara was also there and not very cheerful or nice. And she hadn't been since."

"Do you have any idea what they were talking about?" Ann stirred the glaze while it heated.

"Not really. I was trying to sell tortes, not eavesdrop on a soon-to-be murder scene. But there was definitely a source of tension."

"I hate to be the one to bring it up, but then there's you. Already involved in a previous murder investigation," Charlene stated.

"Oh, nonsense." Kitty huffed. "Holly didn't kill anyone."

"We're being official here," Charlene reminded her, a dot of cheesecake on her nose. "We're looking at it from a cop's perspective."

"Don't remind me," Holly said. "Except there's one huge difference. My cakes weren't used as a weapon this time. Agatha might've died of poison, but it wasn't through the tortes. I just happened to be there. I just happened to be the one to realize Agatha had died when I tried to save her from a stray firework."

"Tell us more about this afternoon." Charlene pointed a wooden spoon at Holly, shaking it. "This time don't leave anything out."

Heat rose in Holly's cheeks at the thought of Trent. She thought about their previous kiss. Any sizzle in their relationship had fizzled out when Trent caught her on the Poppleton property. Taking time to compose her thoughts, Holly poured the cheesecake into the eight-inch pans and the muffins tins. When the trays were in the oven baking, she poured another glass of wine.

"Fine. I'll tell you everything."

She told them about her run-in with Donovan, how he talked about wills and keeping them simple and straightforward. He seemed to be talking from experience. Possibly recent experience. She told them that the will she found in Agatha's desk had seemed to be simple enough. All the children received a portion of the estate, but there didn't seem to be anything beyond that. She told them about the letter from Andrea Givingworth, asking back what at some point had been stolen from them.

Ann tapped her chin, deep in thought.

"What is it?" Charlene asked.

"The will might not be as simple as it looked. Expensive properties with a view and high value often have high property taxes. I'm talking a lot. Often families inherit something that is more expensive to keep than to sell."

Holly jumped in. "So there could be a battle between keeping a house in the family or selling for the cash."

"Right," Ann said. "Whatever cash they can get for it. A house like that is a hard sell these days."

"Definitely a possible motive for murder if tensions run high in the family anyway," Kitty said.

"Great," Holly said. "So both Andrea and the Poppleton children have motives."

Charlene pointed to her. "And it's up to us tomorrow to find any hidden clues."

***

AN HOUR LATER, Holly locked up. She thanked her friends and sent them on their way. Midnight was about to strike,

149

and she was about to turn into a pumpkin. Exhaustion and too many glasses of wine had her ready to sleep through until the party the next day.

The once-crowded sidewalks were empty, only the silent echoes of laughter and footsteps. Trash skittered across the road, a scraping sound that sent her nerves jumping. A slight chill crossed her back. Clouds covered the moon and cast the town into darkness.

She tried to shake it off. Had to be all their talk of murder and guilt. Still, she quickened her pace, ready to be safe in her apartment. At the top of the stairs, Holly came to an abrupt halt. A figure sat slumped in a deck chair, hat pulled low over his face. She stifled a giggle. Someone who meant her harm would not be snoozing on her deck. She crept forward, the broad shoulders and the tips of sandy hair, painted dark, poking out from beneath the heat, bringing relief.

Trent.

THE RELIEF DISAPPEARED, replaced by a sense of foreboding. This couldn't be a good thing. Before waking him, she crouched and studied his face. Eyes closed, stress gone with escape of sleep, he appeared young and innocent. No sign of the tension-filled job of solving a murder, dealing with a renegade society nosing around, or listening to a new chief. His lips looked soft. She fought the desire to lean in and give him a kiss. Instead, she nudged his foot with her toe.

"Trent?"

He startled awake, glanced about to gain a sense of his surroundings, then his gaze settled on her. "Oh, hi. Sorry I didn't mean to fall asleep. I also didn't think you'd be home so late from your little club."

She recognized the suspicion behind his last comment. "I assume you're here to have a go at me, lecture me about minding my own business." She stood firm and crossed her arms. "So go ahead. Do what you have to do."

He sighed, no sign of fight or anger. "I'm not here to lecture you. I've learned it does no good where my mother's concerned." He stopped talking, unable to look her in the eyes.

"What is it?" she said softly, bracing for the worst.

The cop mask slid over his face, the one that could straight shoot the facts, the one that was emotionally separated. "I'm not the kind of a guy to lead a girl on." Holly could swear he was blushing but it was too hard to tell in the dark. "If I kiss a girl, it means I sure as heck mean to follow it up with a date."

Cliffhanger! He'd stopped again. Pressure squeezed Holly's heart.

"But I'm an honest man. That's why I became a cop, to root out the lies and injustice of society, even if it's just in my small corner of the world."

A breeze whispered between them. They were only inches apart but it felt like miles.

"I can't deal with the lies. I can't be put in the position where I lie for you, like today. I let you go. I said nothing. That could cost me my job and my reputation. I don't want to risk that or our friendship, because I know you're too passionate about solving murders, and won't stop, even if I ask you to."

Holly felt the excuses rise up. The investigation involved her. After all, she'd found the body. How could she not follow up on leads? Every article Millicent published tarnished her name, associating her with the crime, even if it was all lies. She couldn't just walk away. Those excuses died on the tip of her tongue. That's not what this was about. She had to respect his decision. It's not like they were engaged to be married. They hadn't even gone on one date—just one kiss!

"I understand," she whispered.

***

THE ALARM BLARED at what seemed like an ungodly hour. Holly rolled over and slammed her hand against the snooze button. A few more minutes of sleep, then she'd be ready for the day.

Muffins whimpered. He barked from the bedroom door. He was a better alarm clock than her alarm. Grumbling, she slipped into yoga pants and a T-shirt. "I'm coming. I'm coming."

With a travel mug of coffee in-hand, Holly led Muffins out into the nippy morning air. "And no, you're staying on the leash. No running away. I can't afford your antics today. Too much to do."

She led Muffins down the sidewalk along Main Street. The first customers, probably on their way to work, were out and about. In half a mile, she turned to head back.

Muffins tugged on his leash.

"Sorry, buddy. Not today." Then she led a brisk pace back home.

At the apartment, she poured food into his bowl and water in his dish. "Big day for me. You'll be on your own today."

She showered and dressed in white capris, a red shirt with her logo on the front, topped with her *Just Cheesecake* apron. Her long red hair she put in a high ponytail and added a red ribbon. Today was not just about impressing the Givingsworth's—and looking for clues to the murder—but it was about impressing the wealthy guests.

Realizing she was about two hours too early, she sat at the table and tried to read another chapter in her mystery novel. Her thoughts kept returning to Trent. She understood why he said what he said. It made her like him all the more. It wasn't easy to meet an honorable guy these days. She thought about the current mystery and the gaps of knowledge that seemed to be missing. What had the Poppletons stolen from Andrea Givingworth and was it worth killing over?

Halfway through the chapter, her head drooped. Ten minutes later, she was out, her face planted in the middle of a good scene.

"Hey! Holly! Open up?" Charlene pounded on the door.

Holly shot straight up and wiped the drool off her book. She glanced at the clock and silently swore. She grabbed her purse and opened the door. "Wow!"

Charlene had combed her hair into a manageable style, pulled back into a ponytail. She wore jeans and the *Just Cheesecake* shirt. Most importantly, she wore sneakers. No yellow boots. With a bit of eye shadow and soft lipstick, she appeared softer around the edges.

Holly let out a whistle. "Don't let the single men catch a look at you today. You might be fighting off dates."

"That's it. Not another word."

Holly nodded. "Not another word."

First, they walked over to *Just Cheesecake*. They loaded the trays of cheesecakes into the refrigerated truck and headed to the outskirts of town. They stopped in the driveway, exactly an hour early.

"Can't believe we made it on time."

"No thanks to you, Sleeping Beauty," Charlene added.

"Okay, let's unload."

Charlene placed a hand on her arm. "Slow down. We've got time. No one knows you're here yet. Their nerves are running high with guests about to arrive. Just saunter in and see what you can hear before they know you're there. After all, you've got the perfect excuse."

"All right." Outside, Holly wiped her hands down her pants. Even though she was supposed to be here, guilt and nerves ate away at her. If they were the killers, then they'd be suspicious.

She crept up to the house to find the door open a crack. Raised voices sounded from right inside the kitchen. Holly hesitated, listening.

At first, Andrea and her husband talked about the typical last-minute tasks to complete before the party started. The vases of flowers needed to be put on the tables outside. The trays of appetizers needed to be put out too. Holly lost hope that they'd talk about anything meaningful.

"Did you bring everything down to the basement?" Andrea asked.

"Yes, dear."

"We can't have anyone wanting a tour of the house or our pesky neighbors stopping by and using it against us."

"Maybe you shouldn't have invited them then," he spit out.

"That would be plain rude," Andrea said, slightly annoyed. "And we have to follow through with the plan."

"Yes, dear."

"They should've found my letter by now. They'll know exactly what I'm talking about. After what they did to our wall, it's the least they owe us."

"Not sure they'll see it that way."

"They should. But, we can't have them pinning that murder on us, though I'm sure they'll try."

Holly stepped back from the door, reeling from their conversation. They had a plan. Something would happen today. They'd invited the Poppletons for a reason. Maybe to finish off what they started? Maybe if Derek and Donovan Poppleton refused to hand over what was stolen, then Andrea had her revenge planned out.

Inching away from the door, Holly knew what they had to do. Check the basement and warn the Poppletons. Possibly stop them from coming to the party. They might want to make an anonymous call to the police too.

She dashed back out to the truck where Charlene waited and banged on her window.

Charlene rolled it down. "Is there another body?"

"No, but there could be." In a rush of words, Holly told Charlene everything she'd overheard. "Should we call Trent?"

Charlene pursed her lips to the side, thinking. She rubbed her chin. She tapped the dashboard. "Not yet. Not until we're sure. He'll just take over. We're exactly what's needed here."

"Should we warn the Poppletons?" Holly asked. "I can scoot over and let them know, in a friendly manner, that if they don't plan on returning whatever they stole, they shouldn't go."

Charlene stepped outside. "I can start setting up and check the basement. Maybe that's where the poison is stored. If I find it, then I'll call Trent."

A thrill ran through Holly. This was what it was all about. Saving people. Solving crime. They'd prevent another crime today just using words, the peaceful way. Maybe she could even talk the Poppletons into a truce, giving back what they stole, and the neighbors could be friends once again.

A rumble sounded from the road. Dust rose as another truck pulled in next to hers.

The Tasty Bite. Pierre drove, and Millicent sat in the front. Ready to cater the party that Holly had hijacked.

18

MILLICENT STARED AT them through the window. Her face went from jaw-dropping shock to anger, her face blooming the color of Valentine frosting. Holly couldn't see past her to Pierre's reaction. He had no idea what had happened.

"Oh, boy," Charlene said. "This should be fun."

Holly expected Charlene to get out of the van and stomp over to confront Millicent, but instead, she stayed inside. She patted her hair. She flipped the visor and peeked in the mirror. She tried to wipe off her lipstick.

"What are you doing?" Holly asked.

"Wiping off this stupid gunk. I look like a clown."

"No." Holly grabbed her hands. "You look like a confident, beautiful woman. Leave it."

A door slammed.

"I'll take care of this. This is all me." Holly walked to the front of the van.

"You!" Millicent pointed a finger at her, like it was a gun. "Thief! I was starting to feel bad about slamming your business in the paper, but it turns out I was right. All this time, you've feigned innocence and friendship. Then you do this. Steal customers from my father."

Pierre stepped out of the driver's side and approached them. For the first time ever, he frowned, his bushy eyebrows lowered, his mouth in a scowl as he took in the scene. Holly's truck. He glanced back and forth between the house and Holly.

"Can we call the cops, Dad?" Millicent said, her words like venom.

Holly thought back to the Fourth. The holiday seemed like years ago, and the murder had distracted Holly from Millicent's antics that night. "You're calling me a thief? That's pretty gutsy of you after you stole from me."

"This party, this event was ours. I don't know how you finagled it, how you even knew about it." She stopped, thinking. "It was the other day when Trent was flirting with me."

Holly about choked on her saliva. "Flirting with you? You wouldn't let the poor guy alone, dripping all over him like a sugary glaze, sticky. Too sweet."

"Ha! You're just jealous." Millicent stuck her perky little nose in the air. "That Trent likes me and not you. We have history. A long history." She drew out the word long, suggesting years.

Pierre finally stepped in. He peered past Holly into her truck, at Charlene. For a moment, his gaze softened, then he cleared his throat and faced his daughter. "Please explain."

"It's obvious, Dad." She sounded like a whiny teenager. "This girl wants everything we have. She's trying to steal our customers. She waltzed into *The Tasty Bite* and jotted down the address and offered the Givingsworths a better deal. Probably the only way she'll ever get business," she added as a side note.

Pierre smiled, a soft smile that held a hint of sadness, like he'd been down this road before. "Not that."

Millicent fiddled with her hair, then jerked into action. "Let's go. We're better than them, and we'll prove it."

"No," Pierre said. "What did this young lady mean by you stole first? You can explain or I'll ask her."

Millicent swallowed, glancing down the road like she wanted to run for it. "It's nothing. We happened to have the same holiday cake design, and she assumes we stole it."

Pierre said nothing but held his ground, a stern gaze directed at his daughter.

"Fine." She crumbled. "I might've seen the design plans but I didn't know for sure she'd use them."

Holly wanted to point out that the designs had been in her apartment at the time Millicent stole her key, which she later used to ruin her cakes for this party.

Charlene finally joined them. Unable to look Pierre in the face, she focused on Millicent. "The only way you could possibly have seen those designs was if you trespassed into Holly's home. And, it just so happens her key went missing, and yesterday afternoon someone broke into her shop and ruined a day's worth of work. Hundreds of dollars destroyed. Never mind the hours put in."

No one said anything. The accusations on both sides electrified the air between them. A stalemate. Holly refused to be a coward. "I apologize Mr. Monroe. Millicent is right. After the Fourth, and my stolen design, I felt justified. But it was wrong." She pointed to the Givingsworth house. "You can do the party. I'll leave peacefully."

She'd give over the party, but she wouldn't leave. She'd head to the Poppletons.

"No," Pierre said.

Millicent gasped. "What? She admitted to everything. We can't let her steal your profit."

He closed his eyes, breathed deep, then looked at Millicent. "That might be true. Yet, she's apologizing. You have yet to act the least bit remorseful. Let's go. Now." He headed back to the driver's side.

"But we can't just leave..."

"Now, Millicent. Before you embarrass yourself even further."

Millicent turned, filled with hate. She spoke low enough so her dad couldn't hear. "I'll get you for this, Holly Hart. Just you wait. I'll bury you and your business." Then she whipped around and flounced back to the truck.

As they pulled away, Holly sagged with relief.

"Good job." Charlene stood next to her. "We'll talk about this later. We've got bigger things to worry about."

164

Guests were starting to arrive.

***

HOLLY STOOD OUTSIDE the Poppleton's front door. She needed a few minutes to gather her scattered thoughts. Charlene was over at the party, setting up. It was Holly's job to be blunt but careful with the Poppletons in hopes that they'd stay home. She knocked several times.

The door whipped open, revealing Donovan, a tie hanging loosely around his neck, his shirt untucked. He ruffled his hair, struggling to find the words.

"Hi, Donovan. I wondered if we could chat for a bit."

He stuttered, stopped, then stuttered again. "Um. Well. You see..."

"I know. The party next door has started. That's what I'm here to talk to you about."

"Could this wait until later?" he asked. "We're making an appearance, then leaving. Still have our own family affairs to deal with."

"I know you've been fighting with the Givingsworths. I know your family stole something that belongs to them. I think you might be in danger."

A cold, hard grimace crossed his face. He waved her inside. "Sorry I can't offer you tea and cookies." He noticed her outfit. "Are you working?"

She nodded. "I'm providing dessert for the party."

"Oh, I see." He led her to the kitchen and sat at the long counter.

Holly slid onto the stool next to him, her mouth dry, her confidence waning. What was she thinking? She didn't know much of anything concerning the families. There's always differing points of view. Sometimes a little truth to both.

He smiled, his focus completely on her.

She swallowed and mustered up the words. "You see. I happened to overhear Andrea talking. I guess she sent you a letter, asking for Agatha to return whatever was stolen."

"Very interesting. I did hear she was a bit senile."

"She didn't seem it when we talked the other day. Maybe if you return it, then this tension between families will be over."

He offered her a sad smile. "That would be nice. I don't know all that much about it. Clara was the one who talked to Mum about it. Over shopping trips and meals. That sort of thing. Unfortunately, she's running late, still in the shower. So maybe another day?"

Holly waited, hoping he'd reveal more.

"I do know the feud has been going on years. Longer than I've been alive. Back to my great granddaddy, I believe. It's always been a source of contention between the families."

His words implied years of resentment. Enough to plant the seeds of revenge in Andrea's heart. Maybe long enough to finally bring someone to the point of passion...or murder.

Holly felt the pressing need to check on Charlene. If they caught her in the basement or nosing around, she could be in serious trouble. "Maybe we should call the police?" she asked softly, more speaking aloud to herself.

He laughed, a little too loud and a little too long. "Nah. Not worth it. After the party, I'll sit down with Andrea and see if we can work something out."

"Really? You will?"

"Sure. Though I can't say it will do any good." He paused, his thoughts elsewhere. "Losing a family member puts a lot in perspective. It's time this feud ended."

"That's wonderful." She hopped off the stool, already feeling lighter. "I need to finish my job."

"Oh, right. I guess I'll see you over there."

"I'll let myself out."

"That would be wonderful."

Outside, Holly paused, thinking back on the conversation. She'd felt success at the time, but it was almost too easy, too quick. Death had a way of bringing the important part of life into perspective. She knew about that firsthand. Anything was possible. She had no reason to doubt Donovan. He'd been nothing but honest and open with her since they met.

Feeling better, having talked herself into a state of confidence, she rushed over to the Givingsworths. In the back, on the outside patio, Charlene had started placing the cheesecakes on the tables. There was still more in the back of the truck.

Guests milled and chatted. Soft music played in the background. The desserts wouldn't last forever. She headed toward the front. The truck was open, cold air seeping out. No sign of anyone.

Where was Charlene?

HOLLY TRIED TO laugh at herself. Now she was just letting her imagination get the better of her, convincing herself that Charlene was in trouble. Bathroom breaks happened, even when catering a party.

Feeling better, Holly went to the truck and pulled out more trays. If Charlene was in the bathroom, why was the door left open? Moving quickly, the need to find her friend rising, she headed to the backyard. She set down trays, barely paying attention to details like she normally would.

The party was in full swing. Guests chatted and laughed. They sipped champagne and cocktails. They divulged in sinful pleasure eating her cheesecake. As it should be.

Andrea moved among her guests, being the polite hostess and talking with everyone. Holly eyed the outdoor patio. Where was her husband? And still no sign of Charlene.

Holly checked inside the house. Silence cloaked the rooms, still and quiet. The perfect time to do a little snooping. Find out more about this feud. Without much effort, she found the downstairs office or den. Leather-bound volumes filled shelves and antique photos of long-gone ancestors lined the walls. Except the wall behind the desk.

A gasp escaped. This feud was much worse than she expected or realized. Something that could spark and fuel a fight for generations. This changed everything. Now everyone was suspect. Even someone as nice as Donovan.

Greed and money could motivate the nicest person to commit the unthinkable.

Instinctively, she pulled her phone from her apron. One missed call and three texts from Kitty. All with subject Urgent. *Get out.* It had been Kitty's job to check the town records. She must've discovered what Holly had stumbled upon. That years ago the Poppletons, through unsavory methods, had claimed acres of land that used to belong to the Givingsworths.

Holly punched in the number for the police station praying Trent would pick up. Instead the stern, commanding voice of Chief Hardy answered.

At the same time, feet scuffed the floor behind her. Holly turned, slipping the phone into her apron, still on.

"You just couldn't let it go, could you? Nosing around in other people's affairs. Playing the hero." Clara, dressed in a slinky blue sundress, decorated with sequins, stood in the doorway, a plate of cheesecake in-hand.

Holly took in Clara's stern but desperate features. The way her hands shook. Her eyes, wild and unchecked. Holly feigned innocent. "Sorry. I never should've tried to convince your brother-in-law to talk with Andrea. I understand some disagreements can't be solved through an easy conversation."

That was why Donovan had been so straightforward. He wasn't about to explain the grudge, the deep-seated resentment, to her, a stranger. It would've taken all afternoon.

Holly spoke again, this time, trying to soothe and calm. "It does seem rather unfair though, don't you agree?" she asked softly.

Clara narrowed her eyes.

"Seems like the land boundaries shouldn't be guesswork. Shouldn't be something that can be taken and given like a child's toy," Holly said.

"Exactly!"

"And Donovan seems too nice to do anything about it, to really stand up for the family, especially after Agatha's passing."

Clara relaxed, her face less stern, less uncaring. "He never wanted to know about his own family. Agatha had to tell me, so I knew the battle that still needed to be fought."

"So the inheritance between all of you doesn't amount to much after property taxes and maintenance."

"Not a penny." Clara blinked back tears. "We needed that," she said, her voice a hoarse whisper. "We were counting on it."

Holly paused. This was new information. This had nothing to do with property lines and land value. This was personal. This was motivation. "What happened?"

A tear slipped down her cheek and dripped off her chin. "We desperately tried to produce an heir, a child. We've been trying for years. We spent every last cent on the latest fertility drugs."

"You hoped money from the inheritance would pay for that?"

Clara laughed, a harsh and mocking sound. "Inheritance? Hardly. I knew enough about owning property with views that it would be more of a burden. It was Agatha. She refused to listen, to loosen the purse strings."

Holly's heart broke for her. She hadn't yet tried to have kids or even thought about marriage, but she could imagine the pain and emotional suffering.

Sirens wailed in the distance, a jarring sound. The noise shocked Clara from her emotional stupor, reminding her of the bitterness and the resentment.

A snarl escaped from Clara. She stepped into the room and shut the door. "You've been so kind and helpful, I thought you might like to have your cake and eat it too." She laughed at her own joke.

"The police will be here any second, Clara. Now's not the time to play games. It will only make things worse."

"Ha! Make things worse." She pulled a pistol from her purse. "Sit down."

Holly sat at Andrea's oak desk. Why did these confrontations always happen in the libraries/offices? She'd make a point never to enter one again.

Clara placed the plate of cheesecake on the table. "Eat it."

"Are you sure you want to do this?" Holly picked up the fork. "I'm not the real threat here." Why had she entered this room alone? Why hadn't she alerted Trent to their plans? Even if they weren't particularly getting along, she could've sent him a text or email letting him know.

"You keep asking questions. You bump into Donovan. You stop by the house. We had cops swinging by more than usual because of you. Because you couldn't leave well enough alone. You cater a party next door. Hardly a coincidence."

Actually, it was, but Holly figured mentioning that wouldn't help the situation.

"And now, you bring the cops out here." She waved the gun at the cheesecake. "Eat the whole thing."

Holly tried a different tactic. Clara was a loose cannon, maybe lost enough, to confess. "So poison, huh? Nice touch. Very subtle. Very Agatha Christie."

"Wasn't it?" Clara smiled. "And it was Andrea's husband who provided it. Which is why after you die of arsenic poisoning, he'll be a suspect. He'll be arrested. Not me! Now eat!"

Holly slid her fork into the cheesecake and brought it to her mouth, her hand shaking. She hesitated and Clara took a step closer. The safety clicked off.

Sirens sounded just outside. Car doors slammed.

"You know. You could confess. You could go for insanity."

"I am not insane!" She leaned over, the gun inches from Holly's face.

Holly took the bite, chewing slowly.

"Another one."

Holly pretended to swallow, storing the cake in the side of her mouth like a chipmunk. She took another bite. This strategy wouldn't last forever. It had to work just until the cops stormed the house. Except it didn't sound like they were entering this one.

They were at the Poppletons.

In a blur of action, someone rushed into the room. With a cast-iron frying pan raised above her head, Charlene swung and hit Clara, who immediately crumbled to the floor.

Holly grabbed the trashcan and spit out the poisoned cheesecake. She wiped her mouth. "Where have you been?"

"Locked in the basement. By accident. But I found the arsenic. At first, I thought it implicated Andrea or her husband. But finally, the old man came downstairs and said that his neighbors had borrowed it, claiming a rat infestation." Charlene looked at Clara. "What's up with her?"

"Infertility."

"Oh." Charlene's face softened. "That can drive a woman mad."

Chief Hardy entered, gun raised, Trent behind her. His face, tight with stress, relaxed as soon as he saw Holly. Seconds later, as if he remembered their previous conversations, he looked away and focused on his job.

Maybe there was a chance. He must still care.

"Okay ladies, why don't you tell me what's going on here before I kick both of you into the can and throw away the key."

"How long you got?" Charlene asked, stifling a laugh.

A WEEK LATER, Holly woke up excited, filled with more enthusiasm than she'd felt for a long time. Between the murders, Millicent's daily articles, her almost-but-failed relationship with Trent, Holly had felt beaten down and discouraged.

But Charlene had pulled through. At their last murder mystery club, she and the girls had spent their precious time brainstorming an event for *Just Cheesecake*. Something that would top the failed Fourth of July plans. This time, they talked in hushed whispers, not putting anything past

Millicent. They wrote nothing on paper. When their plans were cemented, they relaxed with a glass of wine and recounted that day at the Givingsworths.

Chief Hardy, furious with them for playing the role of amateur sleuths, had given them a long lecture on compromising investigations. They should know better.

Turned out though, she had listened to most of the conversation with Clara through Holly's phone in the pocket of her apron. She'd heard the confession and murder attempt on Holly. Minutes later, Kitty had called Trent, spilling the plans for the party. She'd learned about the land grab in the town records and knew the emotions ran deep. Trent contacted Chief Hardy, and together, they raced to the Poppletons. Derek and Donovan had been oblivious to Clara's plans and actions, so they said. Nothing could be proven.

Holly stretched like a cat in the morning sunshine of her front window that overlooked the street. With her hand wrapped around her morning coffee, she smiled. Today, Charlene would pay the piper by wearing the costume Holly had picked out for her.

Checking the time, she startled. "Time to stop daydreaming, Muffins." She put down her mug and picked him up. "And today, you're coming with me. Part of the plans!"

She showered, ate breakfast, and then joined Charlene, Kitty, and Ann at *Just Cheesecake*. From nine to one, they would hold a sidewalk sale. Not just any sidewalk sale though. This sale would include a clown, balloons, a certain dog, face painting, and free samplers. Along with the free samplers, Holly had prepared a postcard showing that for that day only, they could purchase any size cheesecake at twenty percent off. Ann would man the shop. The perfect combination of free and marketing gimmicks to draw the crowds while making sales too. Hopefully.

Charlene sat at the table. "Just tell me. I know I have it coming. You want me to wear the clown costume, don't you?"

Kitty burst out laughing until Charlene glared at her. Ann turned away, her shoulders shaking.

"I always knew you were jealous of my red hair, so I thought the curly wig would be perfect on you. And the splash of color will do wonders for your drab wardrobe." Holly thought again of her desire to set up Charlene on a date. Unfortunately, she hadn't been able to find any man perfect enough.

A knock sounded on the door. Millicent stood on the other side of the glass, unable to hide the frown.

"Terrific," Holly muttered. Just what she needed. At the door, she plastered on a cheerful smile and opened it. "Hello."

Millicent mumbled something, her head down, cheeks pink. She scuffed her toe on the pavement.

"What did you say?"

Pierre stepped up behind her, a source of silent encouragement.

"Do you have a moment? I'd like to talk with you."

"Come on in. Both of you." Holly pulled out a tray of mini cheesecake breakfast tortes and invited them to make a cup of coffee at the Keurig.

"Thanks." Millicent shuffled into the room and took advantage of fiddling around the Keurig.

Pierre entered, observing her shop and the showcase of her pastries. He smiled in what seemed to be approval. "Nice place. I like it."

Joy burst in Holly's heart. To have his approval brought unexpected emotion and her eyes teared up. "Thanks."

Then his gaze landed on Charlene, who suddenly had to sweep the floor. Holly looked back and forth between the two of them. Charlene's nervous behavior and Pierre's unabashed attempt to gain her attention. Why hadn't Holly thought of it before? Pierre, a perfect gentleman, nice and thoughtful, would be a perfect match. Unfortunately, Millicent happened to be his daughter.

When they were all seated at a table, Holly waited patiently for Millicent to talk.

Millicent sipped her coffee and nibbled on a torte. Finally, she drew a breath and spoke. "I'm sorry about stealing your design for the Fourth of July cake. I'm sorry for ruining your cheesecakes."

Her father cleared his throat, encouraging—no telling her—to keep talking.

"I'm at your service today, if you'll have me, to pay off my debt."

"I'm sure I can find something for you to do." Holly and Charlene shared a secret smile. Fortunately, Charlene would get out of wearing the red curly wig, the clown suit, big shoes, and squeaky red nose.

Pierre's deep voice rumbled as he talked. "And I'd love to hang around, help out, and introduce you to the people I know in town."

Holly wanted to gush about this incredibly honorable man. "We'd love to have you. Thanks."

***

LATE THAT NIGHT, Holly relaxed on her couch, in her cozy frog pajamas, with her favorite chocolate chip cheesecake bars and a glass of wine. Muffins curled on her lap. She'd just started her favorite movie when someone knocked on the door.

"Now who could that be, Muffins?" Possibly Charlene. Holly had noticed the shy glances her friend had offered Pierre. Almost like they had a history. One Holly intended to dig up.

She opened the door to find Trent on the doorstep. He was dressed in jeans and a white T-shirt. She didn't want to notice or care, but he looked pretty handsome. The more she got to know him, the more appealing he became.

"I guess you're not here to arrest me." Holly hoped the joke would take.

"Not this time." He smiled. "Thought we could hang out, but if you're busy or about to head to bed..."

"Not at all. I'm about to watch a movie. You're more than welcome to join me."

"Sounds good."

They took a seat on the couch, not too far apart and not too close. Holly could accept friendship. With the murder solved and behind them, anything was possible in the future.

Right before she pressed Play, she said, "Hope you don't mind a good old-fashioned murder mystery." Then she winked, holding back a laugh.

"Not at all. Not at all." He focused on the screen, pretending he didn't get her joke, but the hint of a smile flickered.

THE END

About the Author

Laura Pauling writes about spies, murder, and mystery. She is the author of the Baron & Graystone Mysteries and the Holly Hart Cozy Mystery Series. She loves the puzzle of a whodunnit and witty banter between characters. In her free time, she likes to read, walk, bike, snowshoe, and spend time with family or enjoy coffee with friends. She writes to entertain, experience a great story, explore issues of friendship and forgiveness and...work in her jammies and slippers.

Visit Laura at http://laurapauling.com to sign up for her newsletter or send her a message through the contact tab. Or email her directly at laura@laurapauling.com.